The settling
of
the dust

Philip Wickham

Copyright © 2020 Philip Wickham.
The Settling of the Dust
All moral rights of the author have been asserted.
Set in 10.5pt Palatino Linotype & Century Gothic.
Typeset
by
Mad Goat Media.
A CIP catalogue record for this title is available from the
British Library.

Title:
The Settling of the Dust

Author:
Philip Wickham

Jacket design & Images taken from original watercolour
by
The Author

Additional Illustration on page 172
By
Samuel Yarker

In the interest of the environment, this book has been recycled,
and each time it's got worse.

Acknowledgements

My grateful thanks go out to:

Beth and Stephen Williams
Fiona Sullivan
Harry Potts
M J Smith

The settling of the dust

By the same author:

Fiction

The Summerhouse

Undisclosed Advocate

To Walk in Blue Light

Walking Upside Down

In the Screaming Silence

The Beekeeper

On the Other Side of No Tomorrow

Lime Twigs and Dancing Iguanas

Beyond the Green Shuttered Room

The Avital Shroud

The Squaring of the Circle

Marshmallow Moon *et*
Fleurs de Lumière

In the Silence of Trees

Poetry
Collected Poems

Travel
To Treno Peloponnesus: *A Greek Journey*

for

Lucy

If you take a single twig and snap it,
it breaks easily.
If you bind all the twigs together,
they are impossible to break.
That's family

The settling of the dust

The settling of the dust

Chapter One

April

The lawned area of the graveyard had been freshly mown, giving the air an aromatic sweetness. He closed his eyes, drew a deep breath, exhaled slowly, and drifted back to his childhood: the hypnotic and calming sound of a babbling brook, tripping and gently tumbling over small rocks and stones, their corners and edges worn smooth and round over millennia by the continuous flowing of the stream on its inexorable journey to the river and then on to the sea. Perceptible movement of small catfish and stickleback as they gently move the sediments and gravels in their search for microscopic food. Narrow lanes defined by high hedgerows of Hawthorn, Blackthorn, Ivy and

Honeysuckle, where in early spring, the hauntingly sweet choruses of Blackbird's songs, echo and drift through the clear unpolluted air. Old rustic wooden styles, leading to ancient woodlands with sinuous, meandering paths and trackways, offering a glimpse of undiscovered adventures to come. Softly rustling and meditatively calming summer meadows of bluebells, cowslips and wild grasses of different species and heights; their fronds bending and flowing in slow, rhythmical, undulating waves on a warm gentle breeze. Somewhere unseen in the distance, the sound of children's laughter; and pollen, sweet as scented dewdrops hanging languidly in the motionless air, and where time...seemed to be an irrelevance.

He opened his eyes. In a reverential slow movement of his hand, he moved the remains of the once vibrant flower heads and pea green stems, now yellowed and wilted, to one side and replaced them with a lively fresh bouquet of flowers.

'I thought you might like these my darling. I know you like Lilies, but at the florists this morning these looked *so* wonderful that I thought well...maybe a change today.'

He carefully and lovingly rearranged the assortment of daisies and wildflowers at the base of the headstone. He looked up at the name engraved into the grey Portland limestone, DAISY DERHAM. He touched the stone with his right hand and lowered his head. A single tear slipped from each eye and began to trace the lines of his face. One salty tear ending in the corner of his mouth; the other stops and hangs from his jaw. After a few moments, he stands, gives an affectionate smile and wipes away the tears.

'Well, I have to go now Daisy. Shopping. You'd laugh to see me trying to cook things: over boiling, burning, adding the wrong amounts of, well, *everything* really. It's truly woeful.'

He emitted a small but heartfelt laugh.

'I'll come back to see you soon my darling.'

He is just about to turn to leave when he hears a familiar sound. He looks skywards. Overhead he sees the distinctive V shaped beaded necklace of a wedge of Hooper swans flapping their wings gracefully in harmony. Each individual flying together as one coordinated unit; each honking and constantly communicating with their family members, giving directions and reassuring the others that they are all still safe...all still together with their clan. Leaning awkwardly and a little too far backwards, he stumbles. Unexpectedly, hands gripping his shoulders supported him.

'Are you alright?'

He turns to see the face of a young woman. He estimates her to be in her late twenties, although it's always hard to tell, and if you value your life, better not saying.

'Yes yes. Thank you. That's very kind of you.'

11

'Right place right time. I guess,' she said smiling warmly.

'Absolutely,' he said retuning the smile.

'Worth falling for though,' she added.

He looked slightly puzzled.

'I...erm...'

'The Swans. Beautiful.'

He let out a small chuckle.

'Yes. Absolutely.'

'Well that's two absolutelys. That's a very good outlook for the day.'

She gave him another friendly smile. She looked down at the grave.

'I'm sorry. I'm intruding.'

He smiled and shook his head.

'No. Absolu...' he stopped short of making it three.

She laughed.

'You know; I've never noticed how much I say...*that* word.'

'It's a good word. Positive, self-assured…confident.'

'Hmm. Are you a psychologist?'

'*God* no.' Then she realised where she was. 'Oops sorry. A little bit irreverent there.'

'Irreverent?'

'Saying the word...you know, *God* in that way…here.'

She smiled and nodded her head.

He smiled.

'Oh I imagine that the word God is used quite a lot here.'

Once again she nodded and smiled.

'Hmm. I expect you're right.' Then with a slightly delicate look of puzzlement she asked, 'what made you think that I'm a psychologist?'

He smiled.

'Oh. I don't know really.' He shrugged his shoulders and gave her another smile, 'I just thought...'

He turned, looked down at the headstone, and gave a meaningful affectionate smile.

'My daughter.'

She looked saddened and slightly pained. As she had her back to the headstone she hadn't read what was engraved on it.

'Your daughter?' she said in a lamenting whisper.

He gave a kind, acquiescent nod of his head.

'I'm *so* sorry,' she said reverently.

He let out a small but meaningful sigh, followed by a conciliatory yet graceful smile.

'It's the circle of life. Sometimes however, the circle is ended cruelly...and far too soon. And you never fully recover from the death of your child. Not really.' He looked reflectively momentarily, and then continued, 'you're reminded a lot in this place about life and death. I think because it mostly lies undisturbed, you seem to observe the seasons here more than anywhere else. Late winter into early spring-time, with the re-emergence of snowdrops, bluebells, aconites, then the tulips and daffodils and the flowering shrubs and plants. The air fills with birdsong and nesting begins. Blades of vigorous bottle green grass; unfurling fern fronds, and leaves on trees emerging from ripening swollen buds.

13

And on into the warmth of summer, where there is light at both ends of the day, and everywhere, life is at its greatest. Flowers are at their absolute peak; showy and effervescent, and the aromas and scents hang motionless in the blue, still summer skies. Bees, insects, foxes and the noisy, irritable and eager fledgling birds drop from their nests like restless teenagers wanting to venture out to make their own life journeys. In the evenings the occasional hoot of an owl, and the secret life of the mammals and rodents, is given away by sounds of rustling in the undergrowth. Then we pass into Autumn, where the vigour is less, the daylight hours are diminishing and life begins its irrevocable journey towards sleep. Then to winter, and most of life goes into the retiring room...the place where everything treads water, waiting for what's to come. Then the new year turns which we know will bring constants; but as a writer does each time they sit down to begin a new novel; it will contain their own style in essence, but he or she creates something new; something that has yet to exist. I suppose a new year can also bring with it the same continuous way of life, but it can also offer change and opportunities that have never existed.' He looked around him and continued, 'graveyards are a strange place to be, they are an oasis of calm; comforting and reassuring you that what is inevitable, is also a renewal, that in the end life is really beautiful and precious, and is what we make it.'

He looked at her. She was staring penetratingly at him. 'I'm *so* sorry. I do get carried away with myself.'

She smiled contentedly.

'No. Please don't apologise. Your description, your sentiments, were...lovely. You're very eloquent.'

He gave her a cheeky and youthful mischievous grin.

'You're seeing my good side.'

She returned a warm but sceptical smile.

'Hmm. Your words reminded me very much of my grandmother.'

He realised that being in that place, that oasis of calm, and her saying "reminded me", past tense; that she too had possibly come to visit one of the deceased residents...her grandmother.

'I'm so sorry...I...I didn't think.'

'No. Really, it's OK. I do miss her though.'

He nodded courteously.

'I'm Thomas...Tom.'

She smiled.

'Hello Tom. I'm Lottie.'

He looked a little surprised and raised his eyebrows.

'Are you alright Tom?'

'Yes...yes. It's a beautiful name.' He turned and looked at the daisies at the base of his daughter's headstone, and continued, 'Lilies were my daughter's favourite flowers. But today, I brought daisies.' He shrugged his shoulders and smiled at her once again.

'Hmm. Yes, the Lily is a rather beautiful flower; as is the daisy. Well...they're *all* rather beautiful aren't they.' She smiled and nodded her head with a schoolgirl enthusiasm, and continued, 'you know...flowers.'

He laughed.

'Hmm.'

She looked at him meaningfully and continued, 'I'm not being disrespectful or weird or anything, but I think it's good to hear sincere laughter in a graveyard.'

He smiled cordially.

'Yes. Yes indeed. I'm sure that those at sleep here, would appreciate the sound of laughter instead of the usual mournful moping about.' He quickly looked around him and continued, 'not that I'm being disrespectful or weird.'

She smiled broadly.

'You have a good way of looking at life I think Tom.'

'Well Lottie; don't expect too much from life, then you won't be disappointed.'

They both laughed, and then looked around the cemetery. From the looks of the few people there, it appeared that they did not share their view of happiness in graveyards.

Lottie gave Tom a thoughtful, convivial look.

'This might seem a little out there; but do you fancy a coffee or...'

Tom seemed a little taken-a-back.

She shook her head.

'Well *that* was a little awkward. I'm sorry. I don't know what I was thinking. I...erm. I don't usually pick up strange men in graveyards.'

He laughed.

'Two things: first, that you think I'm a little strange; which is OK by me. Secondly, I think it's a *lovely* idea. Two people, never met. I like that kind of spontaneity.

I'm flattered. Especially after giving you my graveyard observations, whether you wanted to hear them...or not.'

She smiled warmly.

'Not at all unwelcome. I'm very glad you did.'

'The thought of anyone wanting to spend time listening to me eulogising away: me, who was once described by a school teacher as having the personality of a sprig of parsley, is at best brave, at worst, reckless.'

Another sincere smile followed.

'Yeah. A good teacher can turn your life around.' She shook her head and laughed.

He smiled broadly and nodded.

'Yes. That particular teacher certainly turned my life around, albeit inadvertently. I became undeniably clear that I would prove her wrong.'

'And did you Tom?'

He raised his eyebrows and gave her an impish grin. She nodded her head slowly and smiled and continued, 'how about that coffee then?'

'I'd love to. But I have shopping to do and an appointment with...'

'It's OK. *Really.* It was just an idea.'

Tom looked a little lost in thought.

'Are you OK?'

'Yes. It's...well. I can't for the life of me remember who I have an appointment with?'

She looked kindly at him.

'Check your phone.'

'Yes. *Good* idea.'

He removed his phone and scrolled through. He let out a small sigh.

'Nope.'

'Maybe back at your home there's an appointment card or something written down about who you're meeting. If you're anything like me, I have a house full of scraps of paper and post-it notes; none of them join together to make any sense. I sometimes find them in pockets after washing...the ink blurred and smudged. I often wonder what I've missed out on.'

He laughed again and shook his head.

'Yes. I'm sure you're right. I do the same. All those bobbles of paper that takes you forever to pick them out of your clothes.'

She smiled broadly.

'Look. Would you think it a bit weird if I gave you my number? I'd like that coffee sometime.'

He smiled.

'You're right, it is weird. Give me your number.'

They laughed and exchanged their details.

She passed him a meaningful smile.

'It was really nice meeting you Tom.'

'And you Lottie. Not what I expected at all today.'

'Well the unexpected is good. It's a little like your writer; we've created something new...something that wasn't there, but now exists.'

He laughed.

'Oh no! Now there's *two* of us eulogising.'

She laughed.

He gave a broad smile.

'Well. Goodbye Lottie. It was good to meet you. You have added a different perspective to my little day.'
She returned the smile.
'Goodbye Tom.'
She began to walk towards the main gates, then stopped and turned. Quite still, Tom stood and looked at her. She waved, he returned the wave; she turned again, walked out through the large ornate wrought-iron gates and turned right. Tom remained motionless, alone, and deep in thought.
Neither of them knowing that, on that "little day", what course their meeting in the graveyard had set them both on, and of the consequences that were to follow…

Chapter Two

A week later...

Tom was sitting in his small garden admiring the fruits of his labour. Over the seasons and in-between the intermittent showers and sunshine, he had worked hard at achieving his aim of creating a cottage garden herbaceous border. Although seventy-two, he had always looked after himself and led an active life which now, in his later years, afforded him powerful lungs, stamina, good muscle tone and a suppleness that a man half his age would envy. He exhaled a happy and contented sigh. His phone ringing broke his reverie. Although he could hear it, the ring tone was distant and he couldn't for the life of him remember where he'd left it. He searched though his jacket pockets, then his trousers where he found bits of bobbles of washed paper, he then looked around him and underneath the table. The phone stopped ringing.

'Bugger.'

He retraced his steps.

'It must be somewhere here.'

He turned and looked at the border; it was lying in amongst the newly planted Penstemon.

'Ah.'

He picked it up and checked to see who had phoned.

'Lottie?' He looked a little confused momentarily; then, *'Lottie. Right.'*

There was no message. He hesitated, then walked back to the table and sat down in one of the chairs. He wasn't sure why she didn't leave a message. Why do people not leave messages he thought to himself? There could be many reasons. He thought that she might have had second thoughts about speaking to him, as leaving a message implies a response. He hesitated a little longer, then, 'oh life's too short.'

He pressed option 2 and it began to call.

'Hello Tom.'

He couldn't understand why, but his heart fluttered at hearing her voice. It bothered him momentarily.

'Hello. Are you there Tom?'

'Oh. Oh *yes,* sorry. Well, it's nice to hear from you Lottie. Funny really.'

'Why?'

'Why what?'

'Why is it funny?'

'Oh, no…what I mean is. I was just rooting through my trouser pockets…'

'Oh yes,' she said impishly.

'What?'

'Never mind.'

'I was looking for my phone when I pulled out the remnants of a piece of paper.'

'Remnants of paper? I erm…'

'Bobbles. You know.'

A short pause…

'*Ah. Right*! Bobbles, notes in pockets and washing machines. I remember.' She laughed heartily.

'How are you Lottie?'

'I'm good Tom. And you?'

'Yes. Feeling good. Just finished off a new border in my little garden. Still, that's all a bit boring really.'

She laughed.

He was a little taken-a-back.

'What?'

'Guess what I do for a living.'

'You're not a gardener are you?'

'No. I'm not.'

Another slight pause ensued.

He continued, 'oh…it's just that the question was a little misleading there.'

She laughed again.

'Sorry Tom, just playing with you; I have a strange sense of humour.'

'Yes. I picked up on that at our graveyard encounter.'

'Actually, I'm an artist, and I've done a few landscapes, So, partly right.'

'Well how lovely. What kind of medium? You know, oils, pastels…'

'Watercolours mainly, and I draw pen and ink, but increasingly I'm using digital media. I absolutely love it.'

'Ahh. Right…digital. At least you have the talent to actually place brush and pen on paper though. I do like watercolour, I don't know why exactly; I think a landscape watercolour is calming and tranquil. To me at least, watercolour doesn't have the commotion and activity that oils have. They're too fussy for me. Still, as I say, what do I know.'

She laughed.

'Well Tom, I have to tell you that it is just as intricate and complex to work with a brush, pen and digital.'

He laughed.

'Well that's told me.'

There followed a slight hesitant pause in the conversation…

Lottie punctuated the silence, 'I was wondering how you were, and if you still fancied that coffee? I'm presuming here that you live locally to where we met?'

'Yes I do. I live in Dartmouth. Do you live in the area?'

'Dartmouth…that's nice. Yes, Churston.'

'Then coffee with a good looking young woman who stalks men in graveyards and has the weirdest sense of humour…who would say no to that?'

Again she laughed.

'You'd be surprised.'

'Well I don't believe that for one minute.'

'When are you free?'

'I'll just check my diary.' Again a short silence...he continued, 'pretty much free until February two-thousand and twenty-five, when I have a sports massage appointment with my personal trainer. So I can just fit you in.'

She laughed again. He liked her laugh it was an easy, good intentioned and honest laugh.

She continued, 'and I don't believe *that* for one minute.'

'We are a disbelieving pair aren't we.'

'Apparently. OK cool. I'll come over to Dartmouth. How about this Sunday morning; say about eleven?'

'That's good for me.'

'Any preferences.'

'There's something quite beguiling about a woman in a floral patterned dress, Doc Martin boots and a full face beard.'

'Should I be worried?'

'I think you'll be safe enough.'

'And you say *I'm* weird.'

They both laughed.

Lottie continued, 'Beth's Bistro on Lower street. Do you know it?'

'Yes I do. It's nice there, friendly staff and really good food.'

'Well OK then. Eleven?'

'It'll be nice to see you again Lottie,' there was a genuine warmth to his voice.

'Yes. You too Tom.'
'See you on Sunday.'
'Bye Tom.'
She ended the call.

He felt a little strange and uneasy at the flippancy with which he seemed to get along with her so well after just one meeting and two conversations. It was unusual for him, as he had always treated strangers, with a little more distance, initially at least. At times he had thought of himself to be too guarded about his feelings. He just felt so strangely at ease with her. However, for all her joviality, eccentricity and apparent self-confidence, he felt that there was another person hidden discreetly, yet purposely, inside. He recognised it in her…as he did in himself.

Chapter Three

Sunday

Beth's Bistro

Tom looked at the clock on the bistro wall, 11:12. He had a first-date nervousness running through him that he could neither understand or control. He stared down at the table wondering what he was doing waiting for a woman who is in all probability more than half his age...at least that. Then he raised his eyebrows and in a happy acceptance allowed himself a small contented smile.

'Well why not,' he mumbled to himself.

A voice from behind startled him, 'I hope you're not talking to yourself Tom?' It was Lottie.

He turned and smiled.

'I can get away with it at my age.'

She narrowed her eyes and passed him a small yet incandescent smile.

'Hmmm.'

She gave him a small kiss on each cheek and sat down opposite him.

'Sorry I'm late. Something came up this morning that I had to sort out, then park in the Marina, and then get the ferry across. I just can't manage my time. I'm a bit chaotic when it comes to time management.'

'Yes, sorry about that, I should have thought about you having to make your way here, and me just living above the town.'

'It's absolutely no problem. I quite like getting the Lower car ferry.'

'There is the foot passenger ferry.'

'Yes I know, but I quite enjoy walking down the slipway to the car ferry and then watching the tug swing around the ferry pontoon using ropes; it's skilful and almost balletic. I love the view up and down the river Dart from the deck. You are so low in the water that you feel a part of it.'

Tom smiled.

'I don't worry about time really. That people show up at all…I'm grateful.'

Lottie sat back in her chair and gazed at him with a seemingly questioning and curious look and then released another smile.

He returned the smile and continued, 'you look nice. If it's alright for me to say.'

'Other than possibly an extreme feminist, I don't know any woman who wouldn't like to be complimented about how nice they look. Couldn't quite bring my self to do the beardy thing though.'

'Beardy?' Then he remembered and smiled. 'Yeah. *Pity* that.'

'I did manage the floral dress though and…' she raised her left leg. A Doc Martin boot came into view. He gave a hearty laugh. Her floral dress finished just above the knees, and hung loosely. Around her shoulders she wore a relaxed cut, pink merino wool jumper. But it was the non-conformity of her boots that gave her the look of the artist. She continued, 'I know we said coffee, but have you eaten yet?'

'I have, but it was very early this morning. Why, do you fancy something to eat?'

'They do a fabulous Kedgeree.'

'Kedgeree. Well, why not…whilst we're here.'

She smirked.

'Cool.' She pointed at the board displaying a good selection of drinks.

He smiled.

'Surprise me.'

As quick as a flash she slammed her hands on top of the table, *'Boo!'*

The people on the next two tables seemed a little put out by her exclamation and didn't particularly share in the joke.

Tom, although a little startled, smiled and gave a hearty laugh.

'Surprise me. Boo. Yes, good that.'

She smiled broadly.

'Flat white,' he said whilst smiling endlessly.

A young waitress came over to the table.

'Hello. Are you ready to order or would you like a little more time?'

'Yes we're ready I think,' replied Lottie. She looked at Tom. Tom smiled and nodded. She continued, 'we'll have two Kedgeree, a flat white and fresh orange juice for me. Thank you.'

The waitress gave a relaxed easy smile.

'Thank you. Would you like your drinks now or with your Kedgeree?'

Lottie looked at Tom; he smiled and nodded once again in agreement. She continued, 'we'll have them now if that's OK.'

'Certainly.' She smiled, turned and walked towards the kitchen.

As Lottie was giving the order, Tom's earlier schoolboy apprehension was now forgotten and replaced by an affectionate cordiality.

'You said you live above the town?'

'Yes. Quite literally, Above Town.'

She seemed a little confused.

'Sorry. I live on the road which is named, Above Town.'

A realisation came across her face.

'*Ahh right*. Yes, I know where that is. Steep steps up to it. Cracking views of the river from there.'

Tom laughed.

'Steep steps and narrow roads *everywhere* you go in Dartmouth and across the river in Kingswear. Well, you'll know that of course. You're not so far away in Churston.'

'I do know the area but not that well. I only moved here just over three months ago. I'm from St Ives originally.'

'St Ives. How beautif…'

She interjected, 'not that one,' she said consciously.

Tom's eyes widened and with wry, self-assured smile, asked her, 'how do you know which one I was going to say?'

She looked at him inquisitively and returned an impish grin.

'OK. And so, which one do you *think* it is?'

He raised his hand and stroked his chin.

'Well then, let me see now. You obviously thought that I was going to say St Ives in Cornwall,' as he spoke he tried to read her expression…she gave nothing away. He continued, 'but you stopping me mid-flow, so to speak, would suggest that it isn't. However, you could be being very clever in making me think that it is the *other* St Ives, when really, it *is* St Ives in Cornwall?' He shook his head perceptively slowly up and down.

'OK. And which *other* St Ives would that be then?' she asked impishly.

'Ahhh nope. You're not going to catch me out that easily.'

She placed her elbows on the table leaned in towards his face and grinned.

'You don't know where the other St Ives is. Do you?' she said self-assuredly.

He gave a small but affected cough.

'No.'

'Sorry. I didn't quite catch that.'

'I never actually threw anything.'

She laughed, and he laughed also.

'Whenever I tell people where I'm from, they immediately presume it's St Ives in Cornwall. St Ives in Cambridgeshire, near Huntingdon. It *is* beautiful. Just like here, it has a river flowing through it with a lovely old Medieval stone bridge. St Ives is quite old and very quaint in places. It has a fairly low-key village feel about it.'

'It sounds lovely.'

She seemed to drift away momentarily and her attentiveness became a little distant.

'Lottie?'

'Erm, sorry Tom, I just wandered off piste a little. Yes, it is. It's quite pretty.'

'So what brought you here?'

'The lower ferry.'

'Yep. For some reason I was expecting that.'

'A friend was going travelling with her partner for a year, give or take, and she asked if I might like a change of scenery. That if I did, I could maybe house sit for them. It would solve a problem for them and would fit with me at the same time. I was ready for a change of tempo so to speak. I have nothing to tie me to St Ives anymore. So I grabbed the opportunity. It is so beautiful here, and free from stress. So, here I am.'

"nothing to tie me anymore…free from stress" Tom felt an emotional reason for the move, but of course wasn't going to pursue it. He changed tack.

'I know Churston quite well. Where is the house?' Then he realised that it was really none of his business to ask that question. 'I'm sorry I didn't mean to pry.'

She laughed.

'Pry away Tom. It's about half-way down Greenway Road.'

'Well, that *is* a nice area.'

'Toni…Antonia, is pretty well off. Her parents own properties in the UK and abroad. They rent them out. The money thing and private education though, hasn't affected her. I like that about her; she's very much down to earth and thoughtful. I think her parents worked hard to build up the business and struggled at the beginning. They nearly lost everything at one point. I think that's why Toni appreciates what she has.'

'Yes, some people can lose themselves by having a great deal of money. Attitudes to others change; an air of superiority and arrogance can follow in its wake. Not always the case of course, but, I have seen that in some people. That sort of insensitivity and self-importance.'

'Hmm. Yes,' she said thoughtfully. 'Still. Wouldn't mind a little piece of that though all the same…you know, just a slice of that,' she said passing him a rascally smile.

Tom responded with a broad smile.

'Aye.'

'*Aye*?' she smiled.

He seemed a little puzzled and repeated the word, 'Aye.'

She laughed.

'What?'

She smiled reassuringly.

'Nothing Tom: nothing at all.'

The waitress brought the drinks over to the table.

'Your food will be with you in a few minutes.'

'Thank you,' said Tom. Lottie smiled at the waitress.

Tom took a sip of coffee.

'*Ahhh*, that's good. I don't mind admitting that I need caffeine in the morning. I'm something of an addict.' Lottie smiled as Tom returned the cup to its saucer.

The food was brought to the table promptly within the promised "few minutes".

With the Kedgeree finished, which had clearly been enjoyed and appreciated as every morsel had been consumed, the waitress returned to the table.

'Have you both finished?' Tom noticed throughout, that she had politely allowed the customers time to consume and enjoy the food and did not rush them, as so many do in other establishments in the haste to turn-around covers as quickly as possible. He absolutely understands the the need to get numbers through the door, it is after all a business. But there can be a balance between customer comfort and satisfaction and maximising profits. The food was *so* pleasantly delicious, that it deserved an appropriate time to ingest and appreciate it, and that seemed to Tom to be the policy, which enhanced the experience of the diner and thereby enriched the ambiance of the Bistro. The feel of the place, was just right.

'Was everything OK? asked the waitress.'

'It was delightful,' said Lottie.

'Absolutely sublime,' said Tom in agreement. 'You can taste the freshness of the ingredients, and all cooked to perfection.'

'Thank you. That's very kind of you. We take great pride in what we serve our guests. All our food is fresh, sourced locally where possible and is mostly organic. I'll pass on your compliments.' She began to gather up the plates. 'Would you like anything else?'

'I would very much like one of your Bakewell tarts,' said Lottie dreamily.

The waitress smiled and nodded her head.

'It's one of *my* favourites.'

Lottie believed her. So many waiters and waitresses say that when a customer requests an item of food, but they could see from the honesty in her face that she really *did* like the Bakewell tart. She continued, 'would you like fresh cream, clotted cream or ice cream with it?'

'*Fresh* cream please,' said Lottie smiling, not needing to think too hard about it.

The waitress returned the smile, turned around and walked back towards the kitchen.

Within a few moments, the waitress returned. She placed the Bakewell and a small pot of fresh cream on the table in front of Lottie.

'Enjoy.'

She gave them both a warm smile, turned and walked across to another table to take an order from a family of four that had been scrupulously reading through the menu for quite some time.

Lottie looked at Tom and held up the bowl teasingly.

'Are you sure I can't tempt you with a piece?'

He shook his head and smiled contentedly.

'No. Thank you.'

Before she poured over the cream, she broke off a small piece of tart and started to nibble around the edge of it like a hamster.

Tom gave a wide smile.

She looked at him and shrugged her shoulders.

'What?'

Once again he shook his head.

'Nothing.'

He raised the cup to his lips, took another sip of coffee and then replaced the cup to the saucer.

'Ahhh. Lovely.'

He didn't speak to Lottie as she was eating as he didn't want to interrupt her sweet reverie…

A few minutes passed by, and it was all gone.

'That was absolutely sumptuous.'

Tom smiled. Lottie sat back in her chair and looked relaxed. She looked at Tom's wrists.

'So Tom, the time thing?'

He raised his eyebrows.

'Time thing?'

'I notice you don't wear a watch.'

'Is that unusual these days, you know with using mobile phones for everything.'

She shook her head.

'No. It's just that when you mentioned it before, you know about time, it sounded like…oh, I don't know what I'm saying.'

He laughed.

'Well. You are very perceptive. I don't, and haven't worn a watch for many years now.'

'It sounds to me like there's a reason?'

He let out a sigh.

'A watch cannot measure the moment…not *really* quantify it. It passes each second, minute and hour with a calculated contempt. It doesn't embrace a thought, a shared moment of love or passion, an unfurling flower or the quite hushed beat of butterfly wings. It forever counts down with an exactitude, cold precision and soulnessness.'

She sank back into her chair and momentarily looked deep into his eyes with affection, and then she smiled impishly.

'I bet you looked at that clock over there though,' she nodded towards the clock on the wall, 'to see how late I was.' Her smile broadened with an air of knowing she was right. 'You did didn't you Tom. You did that.'

He smiled broadly.

'I might have done. I can't remember.' Nonchalantly he breathed in a deep breath and exhaled slowly.

She laughed.

'I really like the watch and time analogy though.' She nodded sincerely. 'I would agree with that. I think you're absolutely right. It would never have occurred to me to think that way about, well…you know.'

The waitress returned, looked down at the bowl, smiled knowingly and slowly nodded her head in approval.

'Good?'

'Exceptional.'

'Can I get you anything else?'

Lottie looked at Tom, he shook his head.

'Not for me thanks.'

'Or me. I couldn't possibly. Could we have the bill please.'

'Yes of course.' She turned and walked over to a desk in the corner of the bistro.

Lottie looked at Tom and smiled.

'I'll get this,' he said.'

'I'm quite submissive when it come to other people paying for my food.'

He laughed.

She looked at him momentarily, and then asked, 'do you have to be anywhere next?'

Tom shrugged his shoulders.

'No. Not really.'

'You've no bobbles of paper or post-it-notes in your pockets or on your person?'

He laughed.

'No. Not today Lottie.'

'Do you fancy sitting in Bayard's Cove for a few minutes, while the Bakewell settles?'

Tom smiled.

'I think that's a plan.'

They paid the bill, thanked the waitress for the meal and left.

They walked a little way down the street until they came to Bayard's Cove...

They found a vacant bench and sat down.

The Lower car ferry was just pulling away from the slipway as the Kingswear ferry that had almost reached the Dartmouth slipway, was steered in a wide arc pattern at a safe distance to allow the Dartmouth ferry room to manoeuvre its way safely out. Lottie had been right in her description, the whole process of docking and departing was indeed a well rehearsed ballet.

Momentarily silent, they sat staring across the river as the various boats bobbed rhythmically and quite meditatively up and down. Tom looked down the cobbled quayside that passes in front of the old and substantial Merchant houses, towards the castle that sits at the end of the cove. A young boy and a young girl, whom he presumed from their familiarity, to be brother and sister, had arrived early to begin crabbing. A generational, pleasurable pastime; a learned experience handed down from adult to child; an ageless and entertaining pursuit, where time seems to stand still and which becomes a calming and welcome distraction from everyday life. He smiled and turned to look at Lottie. She had been looking at him as he watched the children crabbing. She was smiling amiably.

'I bet you used to crab here didn't you Tom.'

Tom's warm reflective smile brought with it a sudden realisation.

'I'm so sorry Tom. I didn't think.'

He smiled graciously.

'That's OK Lottie. People shouldn't be expected to have to think about every word they speak for fear of upsetting someone. Yes. I did come here crabbing with Daisy. I sometimes come here for a drink in the evening and I hear a young girl cry out when a crab has taken the bait. And it could be Daisy. It's that giddy girl scream and release of pure joy and excitement at one of the simplest and pleasurable of pastimes.'

Lottie tipped her head reverently towards her left shoulder.

'I'm so sorry Tom. I can't begin to imagine what that must feel like.'

He smiled warmly.

'It's alright Lottie. Hearing girls laughter is actually quite comforting. Now it is. It took a very long time to… allow that to happen. I was consumed with anger, grieving and then desolation. Grief is a strange and unfamiliar bedfellow, and I guess each individual deals with it, or not, in their own way. I didn't want anyone to take my pain away, I felt that I should be punished in some way.' Lottie narrowed her eyes questioningly. He smiled and continued, 'there was nothing I, or anyone, could have done for her, but I couldn't shake off that feeling that I *could* have done more.' He shrugged his shoulders in acceptance and stared out across the river momentarily. He turned, looked at Lottie and smiled.

'She liked it here, but her favourite place for crabbing was Warfleet Creek. It's a beautiful spot. It's so tranquil and calm. I would sit seemingly for hours with her.

Time was just an irrelevance,' he paused momentarily, and then continued, 'now though, one of the most popular crabbing places is Dittisham, or Ditsum as the locals call it.'

'I've never been to Dittisham.'

Tom gave a look of surprise.

'Really?'

She smiled and shook her head.

'I've been meaning to go, but just never got round to it.'

'It's at the bottom of your road. Well, if you include the little ferry boat across from Greenway. In fact, Its a lovely walk down to the jetty at Greenway quay. And there's a nice little café there.'

She laughed.

'I know Tom.'

They sat there smiling at each other. Then Tom asked, 'what on earth are you doing spending your precious time with an older person on such a beautiful morning? Shouldn't you be out and about with the younger folk?'

She gave him a companionable, meaningful smile.

'You are a very interesting person Tom. Age has nothing to do with whom you decide to spend your time with. I know a few people of my own age, who could bore for Britain.'

'I've been accused of many things in my life; interesting hasn't really been one of them.'

'Anyone that says, and I quote, "there's something quite beguiling about a woman in a floral patterned dress, Doc Martin boots and a full face beard," has to be worth spending a little time with. Interesting? Yes, I would say so.'

He laughed.

'You need help.'

She passed him an impish smile.

'I'll get help if you promise to go crabbing with me.'

He seemed a little taken-aback. Lottie thought that it might have been a little insensitive having just talked about Daisy and he crabbing together when she was a young girl. She could have kicked herself. She was just about to apologise when Tom beamed a smile.

'OK then. But I want the name of the psychiatrist.'

'You don't trust me?'

'No.'

They both laughed whole-heartedly.

'How's the settling of the Bakewell going?'

She laughed.

'That was *so* delicious, I can't tell you.' Then she realised that what Tom was actually saying was that he wanted to go. 'I'm sorry Tom do you want to go?'

'Will you stop apologising. If I wanted to go, I would say so.'

'No you wouldn't. You're too polite.'

'As I said to you in the graveyard, you're seeing my good side. I'm a man of hidden shallows.'

'Hmmm. You mean depths.'

He nodded his head slowly.

'Shallows.'

'Something tells me that you've seen a lot of life. Been out and about a bit.'

Tom looked thoughtfully.

'A bit. I've been told that I can be annoying these days though; so I ration my public appearances.'

'I'm honoured then.'

'Well yes you are.'

She laughed.

'No one actually said that, did they Tom.'

He smiled wistfully.

'You have a great sense of irony Tom, and the wonderful self-effacing ability to laugh at yourself.'

'You, young lady, are far to perceptive for your age.'

'Just saying as I see.'

He looked at the river, breathed in and exhaled slowly.

'My dad left me with two thoughts in his verbal legacy. Don't take yourself too seriously, and where you can, surround yourself with interesting people.'

She smiled.

'And that's precisely why I'm sat here with you at this moment in time.'

He laughed.

'We're a mixed bunch aren't we.'

'Who?'

'Humans…you know, people.'

'Well, yes we are. Thanks God.'

'Are you religious?'

'Christ no! Sorry that was ironic.'

'If life has taught me anything of value, it's that people are capable of such wonderful and marvellous things, if only they would just once, look up from their lives and view the World a little differently. To have the courage to be, and think otherwise, and, to paraphrase my father again, don't take themselves too seriously. To be remembered, you don't need to have left a financial legacy or have been raised above your own ability by others who know little, if anything, about you. You only need to do something extraordinary, achieve or accomplish something that is thought by others to be a curiosity or a little odd.'

She looked at him the same way as she had when they first met in the graveyard after he had eulogised about life.

'Have you done that Tom. Achieved something extraordinary.'

'No,' he replied with a deadpan blasé expression.

She laughed.

'I don't believe you.'

'Well, there you go.'

He looked across the river to Kingswear; Lottie looked at the side of his face. He could sense her staring at him; he turned to look at her. He smiled kindly and asked in a sincere paternal manner,

'Are you OK?'

She returned the smile.

'Why is it that I feel as though I've known you most of my life.'

He raised his eyebrows.

'We only shared a Kedgeree.'

She laughed and continued, 'and a few graveyard anecdotes.'

He smiled and nodded.

'So we did.'

Once again he looked across to Kingswear as the ferry was pulling away from the slipway. Again he sensed her staring at the side of his face. Without turning to look at her, he said, 'I remember the very first time I saw my wife.' Lottie didn't interrupt him. Reflectively, he continued, 'I was on a Greek island sat in a harbour side café, when in she walked and sat down. I couldn't take my eyes off her. The waitress came over to her table; she exchanged a little conversation, they laughed a little together, and the waitress left her. I wasn't sure that she could sense that I was staring at her, and I knew it was impolite, but I just couldn't stop myself. In silence, as I sat and looked at her across the café bar, I wondered if the left-hand side of her face could possibly be any more beautiful than her right. She was achingly beautiful.'

Momentarily, Lottie sat in silence. He turned, smiled, and continued, 'why on *earth* are you letting me get away with all this reflective sentimentality.'

She smiled playfully.

'Well it's all helping with my digestion. I'm almost ready for another Bakewell.'

He laughed, she shrugged her shoulders and laughed with him.

A youth sat down on the bench that was next to them. He took out his phone and was clearly scrolling through his playlist. The next thing was that his track selection started to fill the air around him with music.

Lottie looked at Tom, and he at her. She began to move her head in time to the music. Tom stared unemotionally at her.

'Do you like music Tom?' she asked, her head now bobbing more animatedly.

'Yes I do.'

'What do you like?'

'Arvo Pärt to Steven Wilson, and anything in-between really.'

Lottie hadn't heard of either of those.

'It sounds like you have quite eclectic tastes Tom.'

'Yes. I guess you was expecting brass band or old time, dance hall music.'

She laughed.

'No Tom. I wasn't at all. *Do* you dance?'

'Yes.'

'Are you any good?'

'Well, when I was a lot younger, a girl I was dancing with at the time, said that I dance like a man searching through his pockets for his car keys. For some inexplicable reason, I looked quite smug and took it as a compliment. Not at all what she meant of course.'

'That good eh.'

'No. It's appallingly bad and not a thing to see before the watershed.'

Once again she laughed.

He nodded his head.

'No. Seriously.'

'Well, I might just have to put that to the test.'

'In Barcelona, when I was in my early twenties, I once said to a prostitute that if I paid her for the hour, would she dance with me on La Ramblas.'

Lottie's mouth fell open and her eyes became huge.

'I had a lot more oomph then of course.'

She laughed.

'You didn't do that Tom?'

'What, didn't ask her or didn't dance with her?'

'Both.'

'I did ask her.'

'What did she say?'

'She kissed me full on the lips, said something undecipherable, yet sensual, smiled, lit a cigarette and walked away giggling. I think she thought I was drunk…or mad.'

'What a fabulous thing that would have been. I'd *loved* to have seen that. It'd be like scene from a film noir.'

'I thought it was quite romantic. I was a little bit like that in those days. Impulsive.'

Once again she laughed.

'I would have paid to see that.'

He gave her a rascally grin which was followed by a deep sigh.

'Well, I don't know what time it is, and I know that I said I didn't have to be anywhere today. I rather think that I didn't have to be anywhere this morning other than meeting up with you for coffee, or Kedgeree as it turned out; but I've this nagging feeling in the vast unused space between my ears, that I do have to be somewhere this afternoon. The details of which, as you hinted at before, may well be in a pocket somewhere in the washing machine.'

She looked at him apologetically.

'I'm sorry for keeping you so long Tom.'

He gave her an honest pleasant smile.

'Don't apologise Lottie. I do have to go though and find out where I'm supposed to be. It's not as though this is the onset of dementia, well, I hope not. I've always been a bit rubbish with memory. Not facts and figures strangely, but everyday socialising...stuff '

She laughed.

'Socialising...stuff?'

He gave her a broad grin.

'Well, *yes. Stuff.* Like names for example. I have always been the same with names of people. Ever since I was at school. Forever putting a name to the wrong face.'

She smiled warmly.

'Well I'm glad you got mine right.'

He looked reflectively at her.

'I wont be as tactless as to say that I would *never* get your name wrong. But, *wait a minute,* I think I just *did,*' he said with a mischievous smile.

She laughed.

'You should go Tom. Check out your washing machine.'

He nodded in agreement and smiled.

'Yes. Although sometimes I think...sod it! Just enjoy the day for what it is. Although, it might antagonise who ever it was I was supposed to meet I guess.' He put his hands up in the air. 'Ahh well.'

She stood up first, smiled and said, 'I have really enjoyed this morning with you Tom.'

He seemed a little surprised. And then smiled.

'Yes. So have I.'

There followed an awkward silence. Tom stood up. Lottie broke the silence, 'I'd very much like to meet up again sometime if that's cool with you.'

He stared unemotionally at her momentarily, before smiling and answering, 'so would I. Perhaps a little more effort into sourcing a beard next time though?'

She laughed.

'No. I don't really think facial hair is my thing. But I wont rule it out completely.'

He raised his eyebrows and shrugged his shoulders.

'Ahh well.'

They walked together to the slipway; the cars had already driven on to the ferry, and the foot passengers began to walk down the slipway.

'Just in time. Good bye Tom. See you later. And thank you for today.' She leaned across and kissed him on his cheek.

He smiled cordially.

'Goodbye Lottie.'

Tom watched her as she walked down the slipway towards the ferry ramp. She got half-way down when she stopped and turned.

'Did you ever tell her your first thoughts of her in that café?'

He smiled tenderly and shook his head slowly from side-to-side. She returned the smile, nodded and continued on to the ferry. The gate was closed, and the ferry slipped gracefully away towards Kingswear. She waved to him, he returned the wave, turned around and headed off towards the many steps leading to Above Town and his home.

At this point of their friendship, the consequences of their first meeting were still unknown. However, the journey they had embarked upon, would reveal answers and disclosures; the implications of which would impact both their lives in very different ways…

Chapter Four

Tom had been searching for the aide-mémoire note about where he had to be that afternoon when his door bell rang. He walked down the five steps leading to his small hallway and his front door. He opened the door.

'Hello Tom.' It was Claire, a neighbour who lives opposite to him.

'Are you alright Tom?'

He looked a little puzzled.

'Hello Claire. Yes…I think so. Why?'

She laughed.

'No. Nothing I was just…you know asking how you are.'

'Oh that's nice. How are you Claire?'

She smiled broadly.

'I'm fine thanks.' She stood looking at him with a fixed apologetic smile, and remained silent.

Then Tom remembered whom he was supposed to be meeting; not in the afternoon, but that morning. He smiled knowingly and nodded his head slowly in recognition of what Claire had come to tell him.

'Grace.'

She raised her eyebrows slightly and nodded.

'Twice.'

He raised his eyebrows, took in a deep breath and exhaled slowly.

'Ahhh.'

'Right.'

'I thought she was coming this afternoon.'

Slowly, she shook her head from side-to-side.

'Ok. Thanks Claire.'

'You're welcome.' She turned to leave, then turned her head back to him, 'you take care Tom.'

He smiled warmly.

'I always try to Claire.'

She returned the smile.

'Yes I know Tom.' She turned, crossed the narrow street, walked through her open door, turned, gave him a small wave and then closed the door behind her.

He closed his door, walked up the small staircase, walked across the landing and on into his kitchen. As he filled his kettle, dreamily he looked out through his window across the river to Kingswear. His contemplation was fragmented by the sound of his doorbell ringing again; the visitor's finger remaining on the button an inordinate amount of time. He placed the kettle calmly back on to its base, switched it on and let out a sigh.

He opened his front door. A woman of later years and little expression, stood waiting.

'Ahh. You're here then,' she said with a hint of sarcasm.

'Apparently. Hello Grace. How are you?' Grace is aged 65 and is Tom's only sibling.

She just stared at him waiting for an apology. Tom stood and gave a schoolboy, impish smile. The apology wasn't forthcoming.

'Well. Are you going to ask me in?'

'I have a choice?'

She let out a theatrical sigh.

'*Twice!* I've been here and climbed those bloody steps, twice.'

'I don't know why you don't come up the road rather than the steps.'

She set him in a scowl.

'I think you're missing the point. *Well?*'

'Oh yes, sorry come in. I've just put the kettle on.'

She hurried passed him, walked straight up the stairs, turned right, down one step and on into the sitting room. Tom let out a small accepting sigh, 'right.' He closed the door and followed behind her into the sitting room.

'I don't know why you haven't got your patio doors open. It's roasting in here. She slid them purposefully open.

'I've not long been in.' Too late he realised what he'd just said.

She fixed him in a stare.

'Yes I know you have only just come in Tom. I am aware of that.'

He raised the palms of his hands.

'Right. Well, that's why the patio doors were closed.'

She narrowed her eyes. He quickly headed off another witticism.

'I'll make the coffee then.'

Grace didn't respond, she stepped out onto the balcony and sat down in one of the chairs awaiting her coffee…

Tom entered the sitting room and carried the two coffees out onto the balcony. He placed Grace's next to her and he sat down on another chair.

'Don't you ever get fed up with this?' she asked.

'With what?'

'This view.'

Tom was puzzled.

'How could *anyone* get "fed up" with this stunning view. People pay a great deal of money for these properties as holiday rentals; just to see this view.'

'I told you years ago, you should rent this place out.'

'It's my home Grace.'

'Think what you could earn. It's far too big for you.'

'I don't need the money.'

She let out a sigh.

'Yes. It's alright for you.'

'Please Grace don't start all that again.'

'What. I'm not allowed to talk now?'

'Your husband made some bad choices. It happens.'

'Yes. Then he went and died on me and left me virtually penniless.'

'It was an unfortunate accident Grace. Accidents happen.'

Her expression changed fleetingly to one of concentrated thought.

'And you're far from penniless Grace. Far from it.'

Her indifferent demeanour returned.

'Your life worked out well for you though didn't it.'

'I worked hard and did well Grace because I made some good life-choice decisions. You can't take that away from me.'

'Hmm.'

'You only have to ask if you need anything…you know that Grace.' Selflessly, Tom had helped his sister out on many occasions, especially since the death of her late husband. He has never assisted her to receive thanks, which is just as well, as appreciation and acknowledgement was never really forthcoming.

'Yes yes. Alright then just drop it.'

He raised his mug and took a sip of coffee.

'Ahh that's nice.'

'So?'

He raised his eyebrows and shrugged.

'So?'

'So, where were you when I was trudging up and down the steps?'

He nearly told Grace about meeting Lottie, but checked himself just in time. He couldn't be doing with entering into explanations as Grace likes to needle away at things. He was at a time of life where he didn't want, or need, complications or hurdles to climb. He kept his answer simple.

'I went for a coffee and a walk. I just lost track of time.'

'You forgot you mean.'

Once again he raised his eyebrows as he raised his mug.

'Hmmm. I thought so,' she said sarcastically.

'So, how have you been Grace? The hospital...you know?'

She let out a sigh.

'Hmm. The Consultant's happy enough with me at the moment.'

'You sound disappointed.'

'What's that supposed to mean?'

'Nothing.'

'I've got one more round of treatment then I should be done. I'll be on medication for the rest of my life of course.'

'Well, if it keeps you alive.'

She just stared at him expressionless.

He raised his eyebrows and took another sip of coffee.

'Why do you do that? She asked.

'Do what?'

'Respond to questions in that interesting way by raising your eyebrows. You've always done that.'

He was just about to do it again, but looked at the drop below his balcony and thought better of it. The mood she was in; she was capable of anything. He gave her a warm smile.

'Let's not fight Grace. There's only the two of us now.'

'Hmm.' She took a sip of coffee and put the mug back onto the table.

A short silence ensued...

'Have you been to see Daisy?' she asked with sincerity.

'Yes. Last week. I placed some flowers there for her.'

She lowered her eyes fleetingly, then looked across the river to the Marina.

'Look at them.'

'Who?'

'They come here and take the place over.'

'Who does. What are you talking about?'

She pointed to a luxury yacht that was sailing out of the Marina. He continued, 'they bring in a lot of money to the area. They keep people employed here. In restaurants and shops, repairs at the Marina, in all kinds of businesses. The place depends on the tourists.'

'Well. I'm just saying.'

Tom was all for a quiet life and didn't want to pursue it.

'Have you eaten?'

She nodded.

'Yes. I had something by the harbour in Brixham.'

'How is your flat?'

'Furnished at last. You should come and visit me then you'll see how it is.'

He nodded.

'Yes. You're right Grace. I will.'

'Hmm. I need the loo.' She stood, turned and headed off to the bathroom. Tom let out a sigh and settled back into his chair, once more enjoying his view as the tranquillity retuned, albeit briefly…

Grace was just passing through the sitting room on her way back to the balcony, when Tom's mobile rang out on the table. She bent down to pick it up and take it to him. Being nosey she looked at the caller's name. Still ringing, she passed it to Tom. He looked at it, and without answering, he placed it on the small table by the side of his chair and looked nonchalantly across the river. Grace looked unswervingly at the side of his face.

'Why didn't you answer it?'

'I'll, erm, I'll ring back later.'

'So?'

'What Grace?' he knew exactly what she had meant by "so?"

'Who's Lottie then?' she asked searchingly.

'You shouldn't do that you know; look at people's private messages.'

'Oh! *Private* is she. I didn't look at a message, I looked at the name.'

'You know what I mean.'

'So?'

'So what?'

'Who is Lottie?'

'A friend.'

'I've never heard of her.'

'Well then. There you go.'

'What does that mean?'

'She's a friend Grace. I don't question you about your friends.'

'I'm not questioning: just interested that's all. Just keeping up with what my big brother is up to.'

'Up to? I'm not up to anything. I don't believe this.'

'I think the man doth protest too much. And that makes it all the more interesting.'

He held his hands up as if in surrender.

'We bumped into each other when I was visiting Daisy. She was visiting her grandmother's grave...I think she was anyway.'

'You think she was?'

'Yes. Well...I presumed she was. It's not the sort of delicate question you ask of a stranger. She mentioned her grandmother, and I didn't wish to pry.'

A short silence fell. Tom could hear her mind working overtime. Then she broke the stillness, 'so, you meet this woman for the first time in a cemetery and you what...gave her your phone number?'

'It wasn't like that. We had a long conversation before we exchanged telephone numbers. I didn't think she would contact me to be honest.'

She looked sceptically unconvinced.

'Hmm. Older woman?'

'Oldish.'

'Oldish?'

'I don't know. I'd say about...I don't like guessing the age of a woman. It's a very precarious thing to do. I always give the wrong answer.'

'It won't affect me. Go on, have a guess.'

'About twenty-seven.' As soon as his words fell from his lips he knew he had opened a can of worms...he could have kicked himself. Her surprised facial expression said it all.

'What? What's the look for?'

'Twenty-seven?'

'About that I'd say; yes.'

Another silence ensued. Then her expression changed.

'And that's where you were this morning. With Lottie.'

'Yes. I was. And before you say it, I did believe that you were coming round this afternoon. I didn't meet with her for coffee and make you walk up and down the steps…twice, on purpose to annoy you.'

'You told me that *you* went for coffee. *You*.'

'I *did* go for a coffee.'

'You didn't mention Lottie.'

'Why would I. You didn't *know* her then.'

'I don't know her now.'

'You know what I mean. Stop splitting hairs.'

'Sorry Tom.' She smirked. Tom was a little-taken-aback. An apology from Grace was part of a limited edition.

'You old dog you.'

'Stop *right* there Grace. She's a lovely kind-hearted girl…woman.'

This time she held her hands up in submission.

'OK OK.' The impish smile returned and Tom knew that he wasn't going to hear the last of it. When Grace dug her claws into something, she was like a budgie with a mirror. He knew she would tell all of her like-minded friends, that he was having an affair with a younger woman.

'You get me all worked up Grace. You've a knack at doing that.'

'It's a skill.'

He narrowed his eyes at her.

'I don't mean to Tom.'

'Rubbish. You're never happier than when you are winding me up and then watching me go. No other person on Earth can do that.'

She gave a small laugh.

'Come on Tom. You know me. I can't help it; I know I do it, but I just can't seem to stop; but there's no venom in me.'

Tom shook his head.

'I don't know Grace…sometimes. Sometimes you just…' he exhaled.

'So, does she live locally?'

He tilted his head back and looked towards the heavens for some divine intervention.

She laughed again.

'OK. No more questions. I promise.'

Tom knew Grace's promises were like piecrust.

'I saw the curtains twitching when I came before.'

Tom knew who she was talking about.

'What do you mean?'

She gave a broad and somewhat sardonic smile.

'Claire…your spy.'

He shook his head and changed tack.

'I have to go to the boat this afternoon.'

'Oh. And I thought you said that you had thought that you were meeting me this afternoon?'

He looked at her with a despairing look.

'I had planned the afternoon to do both: meet you and go to the boat. But that has changed slightly. So I can bring forward what I have to do with the boat.'

She gave him a fixed stare.

'I suppose that means you want me to go then.'

'No. It does not mean that at all. You can stay here if you like until I come back.'

'I could go with you to the boat. You haven't asked me in ages.'

'OK. Come with me then.'

Once again she looked at him expressionlessly.

'I think I've done enough walking today, don't you?'

He smiled empathetically.

'I don't know Grace. You never used to be like this.'

She looked across the river as the ferry was drawing up the slipway at Kingswear.

'You know why Tom,' she said reflectively.

'That was such a long time ago Grace. Life is too short to let a historical pain reach down through the rest of your life.' He was reflecting on Daisy. 'I am reminded of pain each day, but I will not let it rule my existence. Regrets are the past, that if you let them, can cripple you in the present and are such a dreadful waste of time.'

Grace looked at him in silence for a few moments and then said, 'I suppose you'd better be getting off to your boat then. I have to be somewhere this afternoon anyway, so, I won't take up your offer of waiting here for you to get back. If it's all the same.'

Slowly, Tom shook his head from side-to-side.

Grace picked up on the slight despondency.

'I didn't mean it to sound like that. It came out wrong.
I know you meant well. I do have to go though.'
'I'll walk you down to the ferry.'
She gave him a small, but well-intentioned, smile.
'Thank you.'

They walked together down School Steps as they come
out closest to the lower ferry.
At the bottom of the steps, Tom leaned across and gave
Grace a small kiss on her cheek.
'Goodbye Tom,' she said matter-of-factly. 'Give my
regards to Lottie.' Grace continually wanted to have the
last word…and Tom always let her. She turned right
and headed off towards the ferry. Tom once again,
shaking his head slowly in a resignation that no matter
how hard he tried now, or at any future time, Grace
would always feel wounded about what had happened
to her, and that in some small way, he felt that she quite
embraced playing the victim. He was saddened that
their relationship had become, at times, a little difficult
and others, turbulent. What had happened in the past,
had nothing to do whatsoever with him. Yet he
understood that family is sometimes the only release of
pain and frustration and that those closest to you can,
and quite often do, become the innocent recipients of,
in this case, a sibling's misfortune.
A voice from behind snapped him out of his thoughts.
'Hello Tom.' It was Stephan, the skipper of the
Sandpiper, one of two of the Dartmouth-Dittisham
ferries.

'Hello Stephan. Not working today?'

'No. My daughter Alice has just given birth to a baby girl,' he said with the proudest and widest of smiles.

'That's *wonderful* news. Are they both well?'

'Yes. Quite well.' He gave Tom an oddly mischievous look. 'They've chosen a name for her.'

'Yes I expect that would be really helpful,' he replied cheekily.

Stephan laughed.

'What's her name?'

'Grace.'

Tom laughed.

'It's a *lovely* name.'

They laughed together.

'You've just missed my Grace.'

Stephan's eyes widened. Tom smiled broadly.

'She's alright really Stephan. Her bark is worse than her bite.'

He nodded his head.

'I know Tom. I know.'

'That really is great news though. Would you please pass on my congratulation to both of them for me. I'll go and get them a card right now.'

'I will. I'm just off to the hospital. I'd better get going. See you later Tom.'

'Yes. Bye Stephan.'

Stephan had gone a few hurried paces when he stopped and turned, 'Tom.'

'Yes?'

'We'll be having a few drinks tonight at the Dolphin. You're more than welcome to join us.'

He shook his head energetically.

'Yes I will. Thanks Stephan. I appreciate that I'll mention it to Grace shall I?'

Stephan gave him a fixed, slightly panicked stare. Tom looked at him meaningfully...and then burst out laughing.

"I'll see you later Stephan.'

A clear indication of relief set across his face

'Bye Tom. That was good that was.'

Tom gave a small smile and continued on towards the pontoon along the embankment, where his small inflatable tender was tied up.

At the pontoon, he released the rope and pushed off towards his boat, Butterfly.

Chapter Five

Almost a week had passed since his tête-à-tête with Lottie in Bayards Cove. He was just passing underneath the Butterwalk on Duke Street, when his phone rang. He took out his phone and looked at the caller ID; it was Lottie. Once again on seeing her name, a schoolboy nervousness ran through him.

'Hello Lottie. How are you?'

'Hi Tom. I hope you don't mind me calling you after such a short space of time?'

He let out a small meaningful laugh.

'Well, you know my thoughts on time Lottie.'

There was a slight hesitant pause and then a realisation of the conversation about watches, she laughed, 'yes I do Tom. But I also recall you admitting to looking at the clock in Beth's Bistro when I was late.'

Again he laughed.

'I did that didn't I.'

'Well, yes you did Tom.'

He turned the corner into Foss Street. A quaint and narrow thoroughfare with an assemblage of eclectic artist's galleries and artisan shops, the frontages of which are painted in the most vivid and colourful shades. At this time, bunting was strung out across the top of the street giving it a carnival feel.

Lottie continued, 'I was thinking about the crabbing thing.'

Tom's eyes widened and a broad smile set across his face.

'Crabbing?'

'Yes. Well, no, not actually crabbing but the conversation we had.'

'I'm not with you. I mean I remember the conversation, but...'

'I don't want this to sound insensitive, but you talked about Daisy and you going to Warfleet Creek...'

There was a momentary pause before Tom picked up the thread, 'you'd like to go Warfleet Creek, is that what you mean Lottie?'

'Yes Tom, if it wouldn't be too much for you. It just sounded so lovely when you talked about it.'

Tom thought that Lottie wanting to go there after their conversation, could possibly be something to do with loss: as he had lost Daisy, she had lost her grandmother, and being with him there would be a sort of connection to Daisy, and he as a kind of surrogate; which he didn't at all mind if that offered a crumb of comfort. He of course could be wrong. She might just have liked the

70

image of the place that Tom had painted with his words.

'That would be lovely. You've never been there then?'

'No.'

'I just presumed that…yes that's fine Lottie.'

'I know it's short notice but, are you free tomorrow?'

'Yes.'

'Cool. What time is good for you?'

'Well, I'm being mindful this time about you having to park-up and come across the river. How does eleven-thirty sound? Is that too early?'

'Nope. I'm an early bird. Eleven-thirty is good for me. Where shall I meet you?'

'If you give me a call when you get to Kingswear, I'll come down to the ferry slipway and meet you there.'

'Sounds good Tom. See you then. And…thank you.'

'It's a pleasure Lottie. I look forward to it.'

'See you tomorrow then.'

'OK. Bye Lottie.'

He stood in the middle of Foss Street with a mixture of happiness yet with thoughts and some of the words from the conversation with his sister Grace running through his mind…

"'We bumped into each other when I was visiting Daisy. She was visiting her grandmother's grave…I think she was anyway.'

'You think she was? So you meet this woman for the first time
in a cemetery and you what…gave her your phone number?
Hmm. Older woman?'
'Oldish.'
'Oldish?'
'I don't know. I'd say about…I don't like predicting the age
of a woman. I always give the wrong answer.'
'It won't affect me. Go on, have a guess.'
'About twenty-seven.'
'What? What's the look for?'
'Twenty-seven?'
'About that I'd say; yes.'"

He then snapped out of the self-doubt and told himself
that Grace or anyone else would not turn his mind into
thinking that seeing Lottie was anything other than
what it was; companionship and an innocent
friendship…

Chapter Six

Sunday
May

A walk to Warfleet

The following morning, the seagulls on the rooftops below his bedroom window, were exceptionally energetic and vocal: they awoke Tom at 6:17 am. He stretched out his arms and turned his head to look out of the window and across the river. He was never complacent about how fortunate he was to have such stunning views from his house. Although he had earned his money by hard work and good decision making, he never took his life, or where he lived, for granted.

After breakfast, as the weather had promised to be pleasant for most of the day, Tom decided to walk down to the river and sit on one of the many benches placed thoughtfully along the river embankment, and wait for Lottie to call. As he closed his front door and turned, his neighbour Claire was just entering her house with a bag of shopping.

'Morning Tom.'

'Morning Claire. Up early this morning then.'

'You can't waste a day so beautiful as this can you Tom.' The heartfelt sentiment was rhetorical.

'Absolutely.'

'Where you off to then?'

'I'm off to pick Grace up and bring her back here for the day. You can join us for lunch if you like.'

Although clearly trying her best not to show any emotion, the widening of her eyes said it all. Tom let out a laugh.

'I'm just going for a walk Claire.'

She gave him a cheeky grin.

'You're wicked you are.'

He laughed again.

'See you later then.'

'Yes. Enjoy your walk Tom.'

He gave a wave in the air as he set off towards Crowthers Hill. At the bottom of the hill, he turned right and onto Smith Street. At the end of the street, the heady aroma from the Bakery of freshly baked pasties, and pastries made him wish he hadn't had already eaten.

He made his way past the Boat Float and crossed the road opposite Platform 1 restaurant, and made his way to one of the unoccupied benches along the embankment.

The river was meditational and tranquil as an almost imperceptible current carried the water towards the estuary and river mouth where the Dartmouth and Kingswear castles sit; from there it flows out into the English Channel after its journey of 75 kilometres from two sources, West Dart and east Dart Dartmoor.

He let out a slow, deep satisfying sigh. Just then a little further along the embankment, the small red and cream 12 seater Dartmouth to Dittisham ferry, the Carlina, was just leaving. On board were 6 passengers, an excitable Springer Spaniel and two rather large baguettes in a beach bag. Although not having a watch, and rarely using his phone to see the time, Tom knew what time he had left his house, he also knew the constant and regular departure times of the ferry to Dittisham...it was 11am. As it chugged past, the skipper waved to Tom, he smiled and returned the friendly gesture. Sat on a bench to his left, a tourist had ill-advisedly, given a small piece of his pasty to a doleful looking seagull; a learned ploy and one executed with great skill to procure tit-bits from unsuspecting tourists – or grockles as they are sometimes rather tongue-in-cheek called by locals. Tom knew exactly what would happen next. As the downcast seagull continued to pester the man, it only served as a well-rehearsed distraction to the planed collusion as his accomplices carried out their attack. Within the blink of an eye, his pasty was gone. He was left holding a small slice of potato and his face displaying a look of total astonishment. He turned, looked at Tom and raised his arm in the air. Tom smiled convivially and nodded to a sign behind the man's head which read: "Please do not feed the seagulls". Tom shrugged his shoulders and the man nodded his head thoughtfully, brushed a few fallen flakes of pastry from his lap, stood and walked away from the crime scene. The few remnants of pastry were soon gobbled up by a bedraggled, plump, wobbling woodpigeon.

Once again a calmness settled over the place as he continued to enjoy his reverie. A few moments later however, his daydream was interrupted by his phone ringing. It was Lottie.

'Hi Tom. I'm a little early I'm afraid.'

'Hello Lottie. That's OK. I'm down at the river now. Are you in Kingswear?'

'I'm just crossing on the ferry.'

'Right. I'll meet you at the slipway.'

'Cool. Thanks Tom. See you there.'

Lottie was waiting for Tom as he arrived. She walked across to him and kissed him on both cheeks.

'How are you Tom?'

'I'm good Lottie. And how's life been treating you this week?'

She nodded her head energetically.

'Really good this week.'

Tom tipped his head to one side questioningly.

'This week?'

She smiled.

'Well let's just say that until recently, life has treated me a little like a baby treats a nappy.'

'A messy, but interesting analogy.'

She threw her head back and laughed,

'Well, life can be like that occasionally Tom.'

Then she realised that Tom knew that only too well. She gave him an apologetic look.

'Sorry…I didn't mean…'

He laughed.

'*No no*! I agree.'

She continued, 'that's why I enjoy sleeping so much, as my life has a tendency to fall apart when I'm awake.'

'Surely not.'

She gave him an impish smile.

'No. Only kidding. I'm an early riser.' She smiled and linked his arm, but then hesitated as she wasn't sure if Tom would mind the presumption, she asked, 'is it OK Tom?'

'Well, as long as it's not because you feel that I need supporting in some Care in the Community sort of way.'

Once again she let out an honest and whole-hearted laugh.

'We *all* need support at some time in our lives Tom.'

'Amen to that.'

'Do you want to show me your Warfleet Creek then?'
He nodded and smiled.
'If you insist.'
She gave a warm smile.
'I do.'

They set off walking and passed by Beth's Bistro.
'Tempting Tom.'
'It was rather nice wasn't it.'
'Delish.'
Walking up a few steps they left Lower Street and at the top of the steps, turned left on to Newcomen Road. As the road climbed steadily, they came to the back of The Dartmouth Arms.
Lottie nodded her head towards the pub.
'Nice?'
'Yes. It's very cosy inside, especially in winter. Really nice food and drink as well, and pleasant bar staff.'
'I noticed people drinking and eating outside when we sat in Bayards Cove last week.'
Tom looked reflectively.
'Was it really only last week.'
She smiled.
'Yes Tom.'

As the road rose higher the views out across and up and down the river, were picturesque and restful. Lottie stopped momentarily to take in the full panoramic scene of the river and the vista out to sea.
'What a *lovely* place to live,' she said dreamily.

'Do you know what, I never take any of this for granted. Even if I'm having a bad day - and I've had a few of those, I'm always thankful for what I have.'
She looked at him and smiled.
'Yes. I thought you might Tom.'
He laughed.
'What do you mean by that?'
'Oh. Nothing really. Come on.'

They set off walking again passing an eclectic mix of some very exclusive newer properties and older terraced houses, many possibly once owned by the wealthy merchants that Dartmouth produced through its profitable seafaring activities, legal or otherwise. At this point the road changes its name to South Town. A little further on brought them to another road name change, to Warfleet Road, off to their right, Swannaton Road, whose gradient is at best described as challenging.
The footpath at this point followed a gradual decent. As the road and path continued to descend at different levels. A curve to the right, offered the first glimpse of Warfleet Creek on the left hand side.
'Warfleet Creek?' asked Lottie
'Yes,' said Tom as a consummate smile set across his face. 'Warfleet Creek.'
A little further, on the left hand-side of the road, was Castle Road, which as its name implies, leads to Dartmouth Castle. The road took them over and across the top of the creek slipway. A small cluster of high-end

houses lay at the head of the creek with an old mill, now converted into private apartments. As they took a left curve either side of the road was deeply wooded. Tom stopped.

'Just through here Lottie.'

Through a gap in the foliage, a small dirt path snaked off towards the river. It opened out onto a small and very pretty stone revetment terrace where there was an empty bench. They sat down and began to absorb the landscape that lay before them…

After a few minutes Lottie broke the silence, 'it's so lovely here Tom.' She looked at the side of his head, although she knew she had no right, she so wanted to ask him about Daisy. Tom turned and looked at her. He passed her a warm-hearted smile and instinctively he knew.

'She was twenty-four when she died. Nineteen-ninety-seven. A bleed on the brain took Daisy away from me. Not just me of course, but all those lives that she could have touched had she lived. Children she may have had, and their children. Lives that may have altered in some way. Some said afterwards that it was mercifully quick. I know they meant well but, being "quick" gave no time to say the things that she needed to hear before she passed away. How much I cared for her; how much she lit up my World. I sometimes think that she was the reason that I was born. Merciful?' He raised his eyes questioningly. Lottie sat in silence not wanting to interrupt Tom's emotional reflections. He continued, 'this though is not a sad place for me Lottie, it's a happy place. That might sound a little strange, but I feel her here more than anywhere else, and that's comforting.' He paused momentarily. Looking out across the river he watched a solitary seagull sat on top of a vacant mooring buoy, as it moved slowly up and down rhythmically with the pulse of the gentle undulating current of the river. And Lottie watching two swans near to the slipway gracefully preening their feathers. He continued, 'one wet and miserable morning, Daisy's mother walked out of the house, and disappeared from our lives forever.'

Lottie turned and stared once again at the side of his face. He continued to look out across the river, 'to this day, I have never understood why Hellene, my wife, left us. I thought something terrible had happened to her. I made frantic phone calls to friends and family. Nothing. A few days later I received a letter, it had been stamped in London, the letter saying that she felt her love for me wasn't there anymore and rather than hurt Daisy and I later, it was best to leave when she did. She added that she was returning to Greece. She thought that by explaining what she did in that way, I would be so angry that I would want to forget all about her. But I loved her so much and I've felt the pain of that loss ever since. I guess an analogy would be that the amputee still feels the missing limb for years after it has been cut away. Hellene leaving like that, in that way, felt just as surgical. I couldn't find her anywhere. I wasn't even able to tell her that Daisy had died. Hellene's mother was Greek and her father French. I went to her family home in Samos, but her family said that they knew nothing and had not heard from her for quite some time. Everywhere I looked I drew a blank. I seemed to have had all the jigsaw pieces, but the wrong picture was on the box. I eventually had to accept that she had left me for good; not to anguish over the reasons as grief can be a vicious mistress, and get on with the business of bringing up Daisy as best as I possibly could on my own. But even so, never knowing the answer as to why she left us that morning; when I least expect it, still comes back to plague me.

Lottie held his hand tenderly.

'You don't have to continue Tom; I can see how painful it is for you.'

He gave her a heartfelt smile.

'You would have liked Daisy, and I know she would have liked you. No. I don't mind talking about it Lottie.' Once again a short reflective pause before he continued, 'sometimes on a sunny day walking through a woodland, a seam of light can shine through the trees forming a tiger pattered shaft of warm, honey coloured light, where pollen, insects and dust spiral together in a kind of frenetic, yet choreographed, ballet. That's how my life feels sometimes, ordered and content, yet unsettled.' His contemplation was distracted fleetingly by a young woman in a small wooden rowboat out in the creek; the movement of the oars was graceful and the sound of the oar blades moving the water aside was calming and comforting. Lottie spoke in a quiet voice, 'I wish I could help you Tom.'

He turned and smiled convivially.

'Help me? Help me how Lottie?'

'Help you to find a way to settle the dust.'

He gave her a broad smile.

'That's very kind and sweet of you, but there really isn't an answer. And that's OK now.'

They sat in silence for a few minutes before Lottie continued, 'would you allow me to try Tom? I would like to do that for you, if it's possible.'

He looked into her eyes. He hadn't really noticed how strikingly emerald green they were. He knew that there was nothing new she could find, but not wanting to hurt her feelings, 'if you have nothing better to do than sitting on a bench in a creek with an old man, listening to his ramblings and taking up the gauntlet of those ramblings then, who am I to stop that.'

She laughed closely followed by Tom.

'Honestly though Lottie, I'm really not sure what else there is to discover. I tried everything and looked everywhere.'

'Well, without being disrespectful to my betters, there is new technology around these days and more records are available than ever before. Let's see if I can't find the right picture for your jigsaw pieces.' She looked at him meaningfully, 'are you sure you don't mind Tom. I wouldn't want to do it if it would hurt you in any way.'

He smiled.

'What else could there possibly be in this World that could wound me any more than I have been?'

Although he had no idea at the time of saying, but that sentiment, "What else could there possibly be in this world that could wound me any more than I have been?" would come back to haunt him.

They sat at the creek a little while longer before leaving and heading back to Dartmouth. Half-way up the hill, Lottie stopped.

'Oh my days, the views just get better and better.' She was right, the view from the road at that point looking up the river was particularly stunning and they paused for a few moments to take it all in...

At the confluence of Warfleet Road and Swannaton Road, Lottie noticed another road going up a steep incline, the name of which, Above Town.

'Isn't this where you live Tom?'

'Yes.'

'You could leave me here if you like. I can find my way back. It's only one road, although it is a road of many names.'

He laughed.

'Yes it is.' There was a slight thoughtful pause before he continued, 'Look, I was just thinking, would you like a coffee? I make a good coffee, possibly not up to Beth's standard, but, you know, decent enough.'

She took out her phone and looked at the time.

'I'm sorry Lottie. Here's me with all the time in the World...what ever time it is of course. You must have lots of things to be doing.'

She smiled.

'No no. It's just that I have to time the bus right.'

'Bus?'

She looked slightly puzzled.

'Yes bus.'

Tom now looked a little confused. Then she realised that she hadn't told Tom that she had taken the bus earlier that morning...

'Sorry Tom. I came on the bus this morning rather than in the car. And no actually, I really haven't got much to do today, at all really, other than a piece of artwork I'm trying my best to improve on.'

'Ahh. I see.'

There followed another short reflective pause…

'Look how about this. It's a lovely day and as we both have nothing to do, let's do something.'

'Sounds intriguing Tom. Should I be concerned?'

'No. I think as long as you are not wearing a beard, you'll be safe enough.'

She gave a genuine hearty laugh.

'Well OK then. What do you have in mind?'

'Let's have a coffee and some rather nice cake and then I'll sail you up to Greenway quay on Butterfly and you can have a nice walk up the road to your house.'

'You have a boat?'

'Yes. She's small but beautiful. What do you think then?'

Lottie pretended to be unsure and showed it in her expression.

'Hmm. I don't know.' Tom didn't really know what to say next, when she beamed an elfish grin and continued, 'a glass of *wine* and a slice of cake, and you have a deal.'

He giggled.

'A deal it is then.'

They set off up the hill and the views at the top kept coming and coming. The road is narrow and is for the most part only wide enough for one car, although there are a few passing places. As Above Town began its decent Tom stopped.

'OK. Here we are.' As he took out his key from his pocket, Claire's door opened. He smiled, but then his happiness turned to a questioning look. Claire understood.

'No. It's alright Tom, she hasn't been.'

He smiled and nodded.

Lottie looked a little mystified.

'Claire, this is Lottie. Lottie, this is Claire a good friend and neighbour.'

Lottie gave a small wave.

'Hello Claire. Nice to meet you.'

Claire returned the smile.

'And nice to meet you too Lottie.'

Tom continued, 'off anywhere interesting Claire?'

'Dentist.'

'Ahh.'

She laughed and continued, 'only a check-up Tom. I'll see you later.'

'Yes. Ok Claire. I hope it goes well.'

She turned and smiled at Lottie.

'Bye Lottie.'

'Yes, bye Claire.'

Tom entered and Lottie followed behind.

He led her into the dinning room; walked over to the patio doors and slid them open. She came over and stepped out onto the balcony.

'I know I've been using superlatives all day, but, what a *fabulous* view you have Tom.'

He nodded his head in agreement and let out a small sigh.

'I know Lottie. I am very lucky.'

She sat down on one of the chairs. Tom continued, 'White or red?' He said with a schoolboy grin.
'Do you have a chilled white?'
'Absolutely.'
'Great.'
'I'll just be a moment.' He left the balcony and walked to the kitchen. Lottie took in her "fabulous" view.

Tom returned with two glasses of chilled white wine and two slices of sponge cake filled with peaches and cream.
'Out of Bakewell I'm afraid.'
'You'll have to try harder Tom. Simply not good enough.'
He placed the drinks and cake on the small Moroccan mosaic table, and raised his glass.
'Cheers.'
She smiled and reciprocated.
'Cheers.'
'Well this is nice, not something I do usually.'
'What, having a chilled wine in the early afternoon with an amazing woman.'
Tom seemed a little taken-a-back. She gave him a rascally smile followed by a mischievous, guttural laugh. He gave her a knowing smile.
'Hmmm.'

A few moments passed in silence, then Lottie asked, 'it's none of my business, but were you expecting someone to call?'

He looked a little puzzled.

'To call. I'm not sure what you mean?'

'Outside just then with your neighbour Claire. You said...' The penny dropped, 'ahh Grace.'

'Who's ahh Grace?' she asked cheekily.

He winced a little.

'Just Grace. Grace is my sister.' He let out a sigh.

Lottie narrowed her eyes questioningly. He continued, 'Grace is...can be, loving and caring.'

'Can be?'

'Yes. She can be. She can also occasionally be slightly overbearing.' He smiled broadly and rather cheekily at her.

'Why the cheesy smile?' Lottie asked suspiciously.

'Cheesy?'

'Well...you know.'

'She was very interested in you.'

'In me? How...why?'

'I don't know, but for some reason I felt that explaining to Grace how we met and our meeting in Beth's Bistro, might, well, it might have come across a little...you know, felt a little awkward.'

Lottie seemed a little confused.

'Are you embarrassed Tom about seeing me. I hope I don't make you feel uncomfortable or anything?'

'No not at all Lottie. The couple of times that we have met up felt...feel, natural. There is a normality to it.'

She seemed relieved.

'That's good Tom. I feel the same.'

He looked at her.

'I hope you don't mind me saying this, but, it's a nice unexpected friendship I think. And I know I have no right to say that.'

She smiled broadly and nodded her head in unconditional agreement.

'Not that Grace sees it that way of course.'

Lottie laughed.

'Grace is Grace...and that's how it will always be.'

'Perhaps she's looking after your best interests?'

He laughed.

'My best interests...Grace? No I don't think so.'

'Perhaps she thinks I'm after your money...or body.'

'Well, one good ravish would probably see me off, so, two birds with one stone.'

She laughed.

'What a way to go out though! To be remembered in that way.'

'I'd rather be remembered for my longevity. Although I do see the appeal. Christ, if Grace was listening to this conversation I would never hear the last of it.'

'So, tell me about Butterfly.'

'How much detail do you want? Us boaty people, and I know it's not a real word, but us boaty types can bore for England.'

She passed him a cheeky grin.

'Tell me everything.'

'Well then. Butterfly is a Devon Scaffie, which used to be called Drascombe Scaffie but has now reverted back to Original Devon Scaffie. She's just under fifteen-foot long, white and manila deck and hull, a beautifully shaped ash tiller, the beam is five foot nine,' he looked at her, raised his eyebrows questioningly and smiled. She knew what his expression meant, she smiled and nodded for him to continue, 'Sitka spruce spars and the main Terylene sail is a deep blood maroon and when the late afternoon sun catches it, it is a sight to behold. Oh, and it has a rather nice bowsprit. She may be small, but she's fun. She sits so low in the water that you feel you are surfing, although if the river's calm, slow surfing, if you catch my drift and no pun intended.'

She sat back in her chair and smiled.

'Well I'm glad I got the bus today Tom.'

He laughed.

'I used to have a larger sea going yacht, but I much prefer pootling up and down the river these days. It's much more relaxing.'

'How far up river can you go.'

'Totnes.'

'That's quite a distance isn't it?'

'It has an outboard, which is useful if I want a rest or the wind drops. It's three horse power, just in case you needed that extra detail.'

'Can't wait.'

In silence he looked at her and then continued, 'you know what you said about helping me to "settle the dust" and new technology might be available to help you in the search. Is it possible do you think Lottie?'

She nodded.

'Absolutely. I'm not saying that I will find anything new Tom, but I've used it quite a bit for researching my own family history. There are literally millions of records available online, and with permission, most churches allow you to access their baptism, marriage and burial records. Sometimes the local church can reveal more local detail about the parishioners and its residents. It can be fun visiting different locations; chasing up family history.'

'Are you sure you want to spend your time on me like this Lottie?'

'It would be my pleasure.'

He gave her a grateful and heartfelt smile.

'Well alright then. One thing I ask you to do though.'

She narrowed her eyes suspiciously.

'Go on?'

'If we have go to any locations, you know chasing up family stuff, will you wear a beard.'

She gave him a playful grin.

'Only if you wear a wig and high heals.'

'Hmm. OK. But I'll have to buy the wig.'

She leaned forward placed her elbows on the table and rested her chin in the palm of her hands and stared into his eyes.

'Why am I strangely attracted to that image?'

He mirrored her, placed his chin in his palms and narrowed his eyes.

'You need help Lottie. And I can afford to get you that help and support.'

'I'll have a think about that.'

After a further fifteen minutes chatting, they set off for the river, and Butterfly...

Chapter Seven

A sail up river to Ditsum

With Tom skilfully controlling the tiller and the sail catching the slight gentle breeze, they passed by the Higher ferry and on their portside, perched high on the hill overlooking Dartmouth and out to sea, the Britannia Royal Naval College. Lottie sat dreamily at the bowsprit, her hand hanging languidly over the hull and gently skimming and parting the water creating a small effervescent wake. They didn't speak much, they just took in the scene and enjoyed what the river had to offer.

As the main course of the river widened out at Old Mill Creek, on their left they passed by the prettily located Kiln Gate Cottage; secluded, and serenely peaceful.

From this point the river narrowed slightly. To the left and right the banks and steep hillsides are draped in ancient woodland, their canopies reaching dramatically skywards and whose roots are gnarled and snaked along the woodland floor and then down to the high tide watermark where they hung in mid-air awaiting a rising tide and sweet water.

Lottie now leaning back on the mast, closed her eyes.

On a mudflat, a young cormorant perched motionless on a fossilised tree trunk; its wings outstretched, drying in the sunshine as a heron flew overhead, slowly and gracefully flapping its wings rhythmically as it delineated the meandering course of the river as if guiding the way. With a "glug" a fish surfaced fleetingly, but as quickly as it had appeared it was gone. On the river's skin, a few small bubbles and placid ripples were left in signature. All life seemed to be in a symbiosis. The whole picture was one of serenity; a oneness with nature. The sounds, the scents, the visual sequence, the tranquillity; it was utterly delightful and as ever, Tom was consciously seduced by it all. As he sailed into a meander the Dartmouth-Dittisham ferry, Sandpiper, was approaching. The skipper, Stephan, waved to Tom, and Tom acknowledged him with a friendly wave. The sound of the ferry boat's engine interrupted Lottie's musing. Slowly she opened her eyes and turned to look at Tom.

'I can't think of anything I would rather be doing right now, than this Tom. Thank you so much.'

Tom smiled and nodded agreeably.

As he sailed by the Anchor Stone, a thought occurred to him. He wasn't able to put in at the Greenway slipway, he would have to moor at the pontoon in Dittisham and Lottie would have to get the little Dittisham-Greenway ferry across the river.

'I've just remembered Lottie. I can't land you at Greenway. I'll have to tie up at the pontoon in Dittisham.' He pointed to where the pontoon was located. She looked at the row of prettily painted houses by the quayside and then towards the Ferry Boat Inn. To the left of the Inn she saw what looked to her to be a café; which is The Anchor Stone Café. In-between the Anchor Stone café and the Ferry Boat Inn, she could just get a glimpse of a steep narrow road with cottages either side.

'It looks wonderful Tom.'

She let out a laugh.

'I had no idea that this was at the bottom of my road.'

Tom found a place to tie up at the pontoon. There were many children and some adults, crabbing there. As they stepped on to the pontoon, Lottie looked at a young girl with, whom Lottie presumed, her father. She was pointing excitedly to the river. Lottie looked over the edge to see an enormous crab hanging on by its claw to a large knobbly piece of bacon. She thought about Tom and Daisy. She looked up at Tom. No words were needed, he sensed what she was thinking. He nodded sedately and smiled.

'Do you want to have a look at Dittisham whilst we're here?'

'Absolutely.'

As they walked up the jetty Lottie looked over to her left where there is a scattering of cottages by the river bank.

'They are so beautiful Tom.'

He smiled.

'I know. Yes, they are. But just a little bit too out of the way for me.'

'Really.'

'Yep. I like my solitude but I enjoy the company of people.'

They stepped off the jetty and she turned and looked across the river to Greenway.

'I still can't believe that this has been at the bottom of my road all the time. Why didn't I just walk down the

hill? I like to think of myself as adventurous; I've travelled a bit, but never come here. How mad is that.'
Tom laughed.
'We are complacent sometimes at what's around us. It happens. I wouldn't beat yourself up about it.'
She looked at him and laughed.
'What?'
'Nothing. It's just sometimes some of the things you say. I don't know.'
A frown set across his brow.
'I'm not trying to be young again or anything Lottie. It's just that I have a youthful mind.'
'Don't be silly Tom. I said it in an endearing way.' She linked him and continued, 'tell me all about Dittisham.'
'Ditsum.'
'Ditsum?'
'The locals call it Ditsum remember. It's rather quaint if I'm honest, that close-knit familiarity; a sense of belonging. Again though, it's not for me that interdependent closeness. I understand it, and see its benefits, but I think I would find it a little stifling.'
Lottie scratched her head.
'I don't know why, but you keep surprising me.'
'How.'
She laughed.
'I don't know really.'
'Well when you do know, let *me* know will you.'
A young man flanked by two children came out of the Ferry Boat Inn carrying an array of drinks. The man smiled as they passed Tom and Lottie. He turned the

corner and sat on the stone wall with the children by his side.

'How lovely,' she sighed.

'They serve up a nice pint of ale in there,' said Tom.

'We can get a couple of drinks if you want Tom?'

He smiled and shook his head slowly.

'I think it's too close to the wine for me. I've got to sail back,' he hesitated, 'maybe after a walk. We could have a short walk if you're up for that? Then maybe have that drink.'

'That sounds like a plan to me.'

They set off up Manor Street; it's quite narrow and either side there are pretty cottages; a few of which are thatched and most are painted in shades of softly muted, pastel colours and clothed in an array of climbing plants of all descriptions and colours. Most of them also having well-maintained cottage gardens, which in itself is a skill to be able to produce what looks like a naturalistic landscape, when actually it has been carefully and purposely designed. The hill became a lot steeper, where it took a turn to the left then immediately to the right at the top. Further on they came to an area called The Level and within a few more minutes or so, another pub appeared; The Red Lion Inn.

'This looks cosy,' said Lottie.

'Do you want to walk a little further.'

She nodded.

'Yeah, cool.'

They came to a small cul-de-sac; used as a turning place in the road, and stopped to take in the countryside view.

'It's very chocolate box England isn't it Tom.'

'Yes it is. Thankfully there are still some places like this left free from over development and dramatic modernisation. No. That came out wrong. What I mean is, of course we should embrace the future, but we should preserve and maintain the past in places such as this. It is who we are; it is our heritage. This countryside, traditions and landscapes are our legacy to those that are to follow. It shouldn't be wiped out...eradicated.'

'I totally agree with you Tom.'

'I don't mean it in a flag waving sense. But it should be saved. Once it's under concrete, it is lost forever.'

Lottie looked out again at the scene: the old church, thatched cottages, farmstead and ancient hedges lining the narrow lanes.

'You don't need to be a flag waver to support that ideology Tom. You just have to open your eyes and look at it. The true meaning of the word picturesque.'

They stayed a few more minutes before heading back to Manor Street...

Just before they reached the Ferry Boat Inn, Lottie pointed to a lane running off to the left. She looked at the name, The Lane.

'Well that's appropriate.'

'What is?'

She pointed to the sign.

'The Lane. No ambiguity there then.'

Tom smiled.

'It leads to a park by the river.'

'Ooo. That's sounds nice.'

'It's very pleasant.'

She gave him a beam of a smile and looked at him enquiringly. He returned a broad smile.

'Right. Let's go then.'

They followed The Lane as it snaked, twisted and turned. They had just turned yet another bend when an old Vicar came walking towards them. He had the kind of face that really sums up the decline of Christianity and dwindling congregations.

'Hello,' said Tom cheerily and politely.

He nodded, and mumbled something incoherent under his breath, and continued to walk away from them.

Lottie stopped walking and looked back at the vicar.

'What the hell?'

'Can't quite remember if that faith believes in hell or not Lottie.'

'It doesn't take much to say hello.'

Eventually The Lane gave way to a path which spilled out into a broad parkland, the backdrop to which is the river. A few children's swings and a couple of other activities were in a corner of the park, thoughtfully set aside to be used as a play area. They walked towards the river where a few benches were strategically placed to capture the views; they sat down. Once again it gave a different perspective of the river. The Dart at this point is at its widest and sandbanks are exposed at low-tide, which gives an indication of how treacherous the river can be to the uninitiated and inexperienced sailor. Many have been caught out in this stretch of the river. Up river it meanders to the left where a little further on it flows past the pretty village of Stoke Gabriel, then it passes by the sprawling Sharpham Estate, overlooking and running down to the river with its vineyards and other food related business such as cheese making. The river eventually taking you to Totnes.

'I didn't tell you this, but we're quite lucky,' said Tom.
'How do you mean?'
He pointed to his right.
'There's the pontoon and we can take a short cut across the mudflat past Pier House. It's quite a significant tidal-range here. If the tide would have been running high, we would have had to have walked all the way back up the The Lane.
'It wasn't planned then?'
'Nope...it wasn't.'
She smiled.

'Serendipity.'

'Karma,' replied Tom.

She looked at Tom. He continued, 'Hare Krishna.

She set off laughing.

'You kill me. You really do.'

'How about you Lottie?'

'How about me what?'

'What's your story…if you don't mind me asking.'

'Well Tom I do.'

Tom raised his eyebrows and looked like a startled owl caught in a car's headlights.

She gave another hearty laugh.

'Well then…my life. How long have you got?'

He smiled.

'Well, I'm in no particular rush, and you don't have a bus to catch, so…'

She gave Tom a warm but somewhat hesitant smile. 'My mother, Kitty, died when I was very young; she was eighteen years old. I never knew her, and she was never discussed and that's all I've ever known. Nothing more. When I say never spoke about my mum, my grandmother – my mum's mum, did say things about her, but never anything revelatory or informative. Just the occasional sentiment or comparative tit-bit such as "your mother used to do that" or "you do remind me of your mother or "that was your mum's favourite colour" you know, that sort of thing. But if I ever asked any personal questions, she would change the subject. It was taboo. I just got used to it. It was just how it was. She was a grandmother and mother to me, and I loved her. So, that was enough. My grandmother never told *anyone* who my father was; she might not have known herself of course. So, effectively, not long after the umbilical cord was cut severing me from my mother, I became an orphan.' Tom sat in a respectful silence as she continued, 'my grandfather had passed away and my grandmother brought me up on her own. I had a good life as a child. I didn't want for anything. She was loving, caring and she devoted her life to me. I had lost my mum, but she had also lost her daughter, so we had commonality…a bond. We helped and supported each other. She died earlier this year. And I miss her. She never really spoke about her past; it was never up for discussion. I respected that and never asked. We had each other, and that was all we needed. What had gone before, who my father was and my grandmother's past, was unimportant.' She stopped and gave Tom an affectionate smile, and continued, 'to use that word again Tom, serendipity. Our meeting like that in that graveyard: two people who have lost those that have been so significant in their lives.'

Tom returned a caring and thoughtful smile.

'I'm so sorry Lottie. I…I don't really have any words that could possibly reach out and comfort you.'

She held his hand.

Again another warm honest smile.

'I think you might just have found some Tom…right there.'

They sat in silence momentarily. Then a thought started to niggle at Tom. He had thought that Lottie had been in the graveyard to visit her grandmother's grave. However, Lottie had told him that she had only recently moved to the area. There had been a presumption. So why then, was she there that day? It wasn't an appropriate time of course, but he would ask her at a later date; the answer to which would prove to be unexpected and extraordinary.

They sat together a little while longer before walking back to the pontoon. They decided not to stop off at the Ferry Boat Inn for a drink on this occasion but promised each other that they would return another day.

On a wall adjacent to the Ferry Boat Inn there is a large brass bell. Tom walked Lottie over to it.
'You'll like this,' he said with a grin. 'Cover your ears.'
She did as she was asked. Holding the knot at the bottom of the small piece of rope, he pulled it hard towards him; the bell rang out across the river to Greenway.
She gave him a broad gleeful smile.
'I *like* that.'
'Right. Off we go then. They set off down the pontoon. Just as they stepped down on to the lower level, Lottie stopped, turned and looked once more at the river fronted cottages, one in particular, beautifully defined by its thatched roof.
'They are so lovely Tom.'
'You can rent most of them I think. This one here,' he pointed to a white detached house, 'is Cliff Cottage. I've

actually stayed there. It was delightful. Just a few steps away from breakfast at The Anchor Stone Café and handy for a pint or two in the evening at The Ferry Boat Inn. Not too far to wobble back,' he said with that schoolboy grin he gave so often.

'Yep. I can see you there Tom. In fact, I can see *me* there.' She laughed. They continued to walk down the pontoon passing by more children crabbing, and laughing and screaming out in innocent joy.

At the end of the pontoon, he pointed to a wooden hulled boat just leaving the Greenway slipway for the Ditsum pontoon.

Lottie looked at Tom.

'Quite a day Tom.'

Tom smiled.

'And some.'

She laughed.

'What?'

'Nothing Tom. Nothing at all.'

She reached out her arms to hug him. He at first was a little hesitant but then held her as tight as she was holding him. It just what was needed…nothing more and nothing less. It gave some release to them both. Tom knows the value of a hug and gives them freely to his friends, although to his sadness, Grace will not allow him to hug her. As a child she used to be, if anything, the opposite, quite over emotional. Now however, Grace finds great difficulty in showing her emotions. Tom blames what had happened to her all those years ago for her becoming more withdrawn and self-isolated.

Slowly, Lottie released Tom and looked at him affectionately.

'Thank you for today Tom. I really can't thank you enough. I never really talked to anyone about my past. It felt good to do that today. It helped I think. I have enjoyed this so much.'

'I should thank you, for spending your precious time with an ex-convict.'

Lottie raised her eyebrows questioningly.

'What?'

Tom grinned and winked at her. She gave him a knowing look.

'That's OK. It's all part of the rehabilitation therapy programme.'

She looked directly at a man who had just that moment stood next to Tom and whose eyes were so widened that Lottie feared his eyeballs would drop out. She smiled and winked at him. The woman who was with him, ushered him quickly away.

Tom and Lottie both sniggered. Tom continued, 'I think that worked quite well.'

'That was just mad Tom. I wasn't expecting that. You should warn me next time,' she paused momentarily, 'that was a bit presumptuous of me. That is of course, if there might be a next time?'

 Tom smiled.

'I think I would like that very much. And we have promised each other a pint at the Ferry Boat.'

She gave an impish grin.

'Maybe next time we could ask Grace along?'

Tom looked more than a little nervous. She set off laughing as the ferry pulled up at the pontoon. The skipper tied off, and Lottie stepped down into the boat.

'Bye Lottie. It's been a good day.'

She smiled.

'Yes it has Tom. Bye for now.'

A young couple and their two children with buckets and crabbing lines in hand boarded also. Lottie sat smiling at Tom and he back to her as the ferry cast off and went on its way towards Greenway. Tom waited until the ferry had docked on the other side and Lottie disembarked. At the top of the stone steps, she put her hand across the top of her eyebrows to shield the sun from her eyes. She spotted Tom and waved. He returned the wave. She turned around, walked up the hill, and she was gone.

Tom walked back up the pontoon to where Butterfly was tied.

On the sail back to Dartmouth Tom reflected on the day. So much had been said, and yet he felt so much was left unsaid. The journey had begun, and with Lottie's help, the jigsaw pieces were hopefully to find the correct picture and maybe the dust could finally settle. In life however, and sometimes painfully, optimistic expectations can turn out to be the antithesis...

Chapter Eight

Dreams, boats and trains

The following morning found Tom having a coffee on his balcony. He could clearly recall the dream that had woke him so early: a surreal dream that was bewildering and slightly disconcerting. In the dream he was in a brilliantly white, seemingly sterile room. He was sat on a sofa with nothing else whatsoever in the room. The luminescence so bright that he had to narrow his eyes. Slowly his pupils adjusted and he began to make out where he was: it was his sitting room. He couldn't raise himself or move from the sofa, he was sat in a sort of trance. Then a figure appeared; it was him as a 6 years old boy. The vision of his younger self walked in front of Tom, and then the illusionary child seemed to fade away. There followed another older child. Once again it was him aged 16 years; he even recognised the clothing as his at that age. Then he too faded. Neither of the visions looked at Tom; it was as if they were passing through another time. The next, was him at 25 years…then 40 years…then 65 years and then the strangest of all the visions. The sound of a gently crying baby. He turned his head to look in the direction of where the sound emanated. In the corner was a baby's cot, also a brilliant white. Without physically leaving his chair, Tom's spirit rose, moved seamlessly across the room and looked down on the baby from above. The baby ceased crying, looked directly at Tom smiled and gurgled…and the dream ended.

He let out a sigh and shook his head. It had rained on and off throughout the night, but the morning appeared to be cheering up somewhat. A few scattered clouds remained but for the most part it was clear. As the sun caught the left hand side of his face, he closed his eyes and enjoyed the sounds of the river: a few yachts and various other craft; most of which were heading out to sea for a day's sail, each of their engines with varying pitches. Tom likes the sound of the engines, the constant drone makes him feel relaxed and thought that each crew member will have the calmness, yet, exhilarating pleasure of what their voyage will bring as the day unfurls. Then to his right. He hears a deeper and more resonant sound. It is one of the local trawlers returning with the day's catch; most of which will be plated up and served in the local restaurants that day. His contemplation is distracted by the seagulls.

Once one started, it becomes a chorus: squawking, squealing, laughing, all building to a crescendo before settling down down: crooning, grunting, cooing and purring. Although distracted, he could hear the Lower ferry's ramp scraping its way up the slipway. He knew from the length of the sound that it was a low-tide. Then just below his balcony on a rooftop, the sound of a pair of Jackdaws gently chattering and cackling to each other. He likes Jackdaws, the male and female partners are loyal, very attentive and caring to each other. This tranquillity however, is abruptly interrupted by a very different and distinctive sound. *"Kaaaarr kaaaarr kaaaarr."* He opened his eyes to see another Jackdaw further along the roof. This was an unwanted visitor and the pair were letting it know. Their warning cry disturbed a Blackbird that he had heard singing gracefully earlier in a tree in a nearby garden. It flew out at speed and let out a disgruntled high-pitch squeal as it flew low over the Jackdaws.

Although the short meditation on his balcony had helped, he had decided to clear his head from his illusory dream, by way of a walk.

He called in at the bakery and bought a rather large croissant. He then took a slow walk along the embankment towards the Higher ferry. The Higher ferry, also known as the Dartmouth-Kingswear Floating Bridge, is very unlike the Lower ferry in that it is hauled across by underwater cables. The cables are only seen where they break the river line on the slipways. When in motion, the ferry is also surprisingly quiet for its size. Tom boarded via the clearly defined foot passenger lane. He leaned over the ferry's rail and took in the view down river. He could see Butterfly at her mooring, and he let out a small pleasing sigh.

The ferry pulled away from Dartmouth for Kingswear. A voice came from behind Tom.

'Hello Tom.' It was one of the ferry boat's crew. He held out his card reader.

Tom turned around.

'Hello Dave.' He reached into his pocket and took out his ferry pass, top-up card. Tom placed it on the card reader.

'Thanks Tom. You've fifteen left.'

'Thank you Dave. How are you today?'

'Oh I'm well enough thanks. How are things with you?'

Tom nodded his head and smiled broadly.

'Yep. Things are tickety-boo at the moment.'

Dave laughed.

'You'll have to give me her name.'

Tom looked a little puzzled, then the penny dropped.

'I couldn't possibly Dave. Not only that, Jean would tear you limb from limb.'

Dave raised his eyebrows.

'No doubt about that!' He laughed.

After a few minutes, the ferry slid gracefully up the slipway, Dave opened the gates and Tom disembarked.

'See you later then Tom.'

'Yes. See you later Dave.'

He walked a few paces towards the railway crossing of the Paignton-Kingswear steam railway, but just before the level crossing gates, he turned right on to a narrow dirt path. This path runs the length of the railway line and river's edge to Mill Creek and Kingswear Marina. Of all the walks he takes, after Above Town to Dartmouth Castle, this walk is his second favourite. He walked about half the length of the path when he came to a riverside bench, it's located in one of the few wider places on the path. He sat down and took in the view. Being morning, Dartmouth was bathed in sunshine, but although Kingswear was in the shade, the air was still and warm. He sat and watched the boats bobbing up and down almost hypnotically by their moorings, as a wooden hulled racing boat crewed by a group of 8 girls, went quickly by as the coxswain or "coxie" expertly steered the boat whilst shouting out instructions to the crew who were rowing their hearts out. He admired their skill and energy, that level of youthful energy, that slowly dissipates with age. Tom doesn't mind not being able to do the things he could when younger. He actually embraces the change of pace. He had spent most of his working life in frenetic activities. First in his job, then later his own company business took him around the World. No, Tom has welcomed each age of change and was grateful that when he was younger, and fortunate enough to be fit and healthy, to use that get-up-and-go and not squander it away before it was too late, as so many do.

A calmness returned to the river. He opened his bag and took out the croissant. He nibbled one end and recalled how Lottie had nibbled around the edge of her Bakewell tart like a hamster. He chuckled to himself. Just then the warning signal pips from the level crossing sounded out. The Steam train was approaching Kingswear. He turned and looked behind him up the line towards the Higher ferry. In the distance, he could see the mixture of smoke and steam rising through the woodland and up above the tree canopy. Within a few minutes it was approaching him. He recalled a tourist a few years back, who thinking Tom to be a train spotter whilst stood next to him by the wall over-looking the railway station at Kingswear, had asked him, if he liked trains, to which Tom had replied, "I used to, but the down-side now is that there are too many reflections in windows for a man of my age and looks." Tom of course was being light-hearted, the tourist however, seemed a little disturbed by his comment, and started to edge away slowly. Clearly not the response he was expecting. Tom chuckled once again to himself. He waited for the train to approach…

As the train clunked and hissed by, the driver waved to him, he didn't know Tom of course, he was just being courteous and waved at many of the interested onlookers and steam enthusiasts that the train passed on the course of its journey several times a day.
He watched as it continued on to Kingswear station passing over the Marina level crossing then under the

footbridge and finally pulling into the station, and with a well-practiced accuracy, coming to a halt at the platform. Nostalgia and childlike wonder, enthusiastic adults and excited children are pleasantly, at that one moment in time, of the same age.

Once again, a calmness...

After a little more time sat by the river Tom stood, brushed off some of the remaining flakes of croissant and continued his short walk to the Marina...

As he approached the railway crossing at the Marina, the barriers were down indicating that the train was about to depart for Paignton. The engine got under-steam, the connecting rods began to push and pull, and the wheels began to turn. The train passed slowly by with a few of the passengers waving to a woman and a young girl who was waiting with Tom to cross the railway line into the car park. The young girl waved excitedly back at the passengers. The barriers lifted and they crossed together. A voice from behind startled him.

'Hi Tom.' It was Alfie, one of the Marina staff.

'Hello Alfie. How are you?'

'I'm good thanks…and you?'

'Yes I'm fine. Actually, I'm glad I bumped into you Alfie.'

'Oh?'

'I took Butterfly out for a sail yesterday and she didn't seem quite right.'

'In what way?'

'The engine seemed to be not getting a smooth flow of fuel. Maybe a blockage somewhere. I don't know. What do you think?'

'Is it emitting any smoke?'

'No. Not really. I was thinking of dropping it in at the Marine repair centre.'

'Drop it off at my garage at home. I'll give it a quick look over for you. It might just need a good clean.'

'No. I didn't mean to ask you to repair it Alfie. I…'

Alfie laughed good-naturedly.

'It's not a problem Tom. Just drop it off. If I'm not in, just lift up the garage door. It's never locked.'

'Well, if you're sure.'

'Tom.'

'Ok. Thanks Alfie. I do appreciate that.'

'My pleasure. Where are you off to?'

'Just had a short walk from the Higher ferry.'

'Nice day for it.'

'Aye.'

'Are you heading back over to Dartmouth now then?'

Tom looked around him. He didn't want to end his walk just yet.

'No. I think I'll have a walk along the creek to the park.'

What he meant was, a walk along Waterhead Creek to the park, and then continue up to the cemetery to visit Daisy.

Alfie of course, guessed the reason behind his walk.

'Nice. Well, enjoy your walk Tom. I'd better get back to it. See you later. And drop that engine off.'

'I will. Thanks Alfie.'

Tom followed the woodland path as it delineated Waterhead Creek to his left. It's a very pleasant short walk taking you away from the road and traffic. The riverside path eventually leading out into a small and pretty park area. He walked through the park to a wooden barred gate and joined Brixham Road. The road being quite hazardous for pedestrians at this point as it carries the traffic from the ferry, but he had travelled it both by car and on foot often enough and knew that the volume of traffic tended mainly to come grouped together; so the walk could be timed more or less to the emptying of the Lower ferry.

He passed a small cluster of modern cottage style houses and eventually came to the junction of Higher Contour Road. It was just a case of taking great care in crossing the road as it runs around a bling bend. He crossed over the road safely, walked on through the gate and passing the caretakers lodge, he entered the cemetery. As the graveyard opened out, he could see a person seemingly stood next to, or at, Daisy's grave.

The closer he got he recognised who it was.

'Grace?' he said questioningly.

His voice made her physically jump.

'*Christ!*' The realising what she had said and where she was, she recanted. 'I'm sorry, I didn't mean to say that. You scared me Tom.'

'I'm sorry Grace.'

There was an awkward momentary silence. Then she continued, 'I come here when I can. To visit her. Just to talk to her…you know.'

He smiled tenderly.

'That's very kind of you Grace.'

'I know you come often, but, as I said, it's a little more difficult for me to get here by bus. The council in its wisdom expecting all its citizens to have their own transport. I mean why don't they consider that the elderly who want to visit their loved ones are unable to because they haven't put a simple thing like a bus stop here. I mean…I ask you.'

'Grace,' he said in a soft conciliatory voice, 'thank you for coming to see her.'

On his walk through the woodland by the creek, Tom had gathered a few wildflowers. He went down on one knee and placed them lovingly at the base of her headstone.

'I thought you might like these Daisy. They're not bought from the florist, as I didn't plan to come today, but they are from nature, that I know you cared so very much about.' He touched and held her headstone for a few seconds and then stood. He turned. Grace had tears in her eyes that although clearly trying her best to, could not contain them within her eyelids. They began to spill over the rims and ran in gentle rivulets along the lines of her face. Tom went over to her and hugged her. It was a first. She had, after the death of her husband, developed an aversion to any form of physical feeling.

'I miss her so much Tom.'

'As do I Grace.'

Tom released her from his embrace. He pointed to a freshly painted, wrought iron bench that was placed thoughtfully surrounded by a well-stocked and well-tended flower border.

'Come on, let's sit down for a few moments.'

She nodded in a quiet agreement.

After a few minutes contemplation, Grace punctuated the silence.

'I know what you think of me Tom.'

Tom let out a small disenchanted sigh.

'Not here Grace, not in this place.'

'It's because we are here in this place Tom, that I want to say something that should have been said many years ago. After leaving your house the last time we met, as I was waiting for the bus, I had a...' she paused and looked around the graveyard at all the lives that had ended, some of whom, whose regrets were buried with them without settlement, and continued, 'I had a kind of realisation; an Epiphany you could call it I suppose,' she nodded her head slowly, 'yes, epiphany, an appropriate word for sitting in this place I would say. I have been unfair and quite unnecessarily unpleasant to you over the past few years and you haven't deserved that. I don't know why it came to me there, at that bus stop; it just did,' she looked at him apologetically, 'In my mind I went over what you said about when we were children. They were happy times Tom and I no longer want to have regrets, as you said, regrets cripple you in the present. Or something like that, I can't quite remember the exact words, but I think it was *that* realisation and coming here today, that...' she paused again and looked at Tom, then continued, 'that I would like to make a new start. If you'll let me.'

Tom passed her an affectionate smile.

'I never gave up on you Grace. No matter how challenging you have been, you will always be my sister, and I love you dearly.'

She smiled warmly, which slowly, but perceptibly changed to a more mischievous expression. Tom narrowed his eyes. She continued, 'so, how is Lottie then?'

He laughed, and she smiling and nodding her head meaningfully. Not for the first time had Tom laughed in the cemetery, the last time was when he met Lottie. She continued, 'it will take time though Tom. It's a habit I've gotten quite used too.'

'So, you'll still be winding me up and watching me go for a little while longer then?'

'Yes. I'm afraid so.'

'Right.'

'So?'

'So?'

'How is she...your mystery friend.'

'She's fine.'

'That's it?'

'Yep.'

'Look. I'm going to be bending over backwards to be nice to you. That is going to be difficult. The least you can do is tell me what's going on?' She gave him an enquiring, yet, impish grin.

'Well, the way I see it is that I can only help you by not feeding that habit.'

'How does that work?'

'Well, for example...' She interjected, 'forget it. It doesn't matter. You're only going to confuse me and shatter my epiphany.'

'I can't think of anything worse, than a shattered epiphany.'

'Oh I could come up with a few suggestions,' she said narrowing her eyes.

Tom smiled.

'Lottie is a very pleasant, clever and witty young woman. We are good company…and that's all there is to it Grace. Nothing more, nothing less. She's a friend.'

Grace decided to let it go…for now at least. Tom continued, 'I've just thought. Did you walk here from the banjo?'

'The banjo? What's the banjo when it's at home?'

'The bus terminus in Kingswear. It's the shape of a banjo.'

'I never knew it was called that.'

'Right, well then.'

'No. The bus driver very kindly stopped at the lodge gate and let me off. It's not the first time the driver has done that. It's very kind of them to do that. I do have to walk back though.'

'You don't walk along the Higher Road do you?'

'No. I walk back down Brixham Road.'

'How are things at the hospital?'

She tutted.

'Doctors. What do they know.'

Tom shook his head, smiled pacifyingly and continued, 'there's a nice little walk through the woodland to the Marina.'

'And why would I want to be going to the Marina? I mean does the bus stop there?' She rubbed her chin theatrically and continued, 'why, no it doesn't, does it.

It stops at the *banjo*. And as I don't have a boat, a walk to the Marina would be a waste of my precious time.'
He smiled.
'Ahh there you are. Welcome back Grace.'
She raised her eyebrows and then a broad smile set across her face. She relented.
'However, as we are here together. Perhaps you can show me this walk then. I presume you haven't driven here as I've not heard any cars pull into the lodge whilst I've been here.'
'No. I walked. Come on. I'll show you how you can get to the Marina through the woodland should you ever buy yourself a yacht.'
'Hmm.'

They set off down Brixham Road where Tom retraced his steps along the woodland path with the creek now on their right hand side. Grace enjoyed the walk and saw a very different view of the creek from that of the road. She thought it beautiful and although she didn't say, she was grateful to Tom for showing her. At the banjo, they said their goodbyes. Tom left Grace to wait for her bus and he walked down the road to the slipway to wait for the ferry to take him back to Dartmouth.

The day had turned out to be pleasantly surprising, and as Lottie might say, serendipitous. Once again, a chance meeting in a graveyard where lives once lived, has ended, ironically, each chance meeting had created a new beginning. On the ferry, Tom looked cheerfully forward to meeting up with a few friends later that evening for a pint or two at the Dolphin. His optimism however, would be dampened dramatically on the hearing of some dreadful news...

Chapter Nine

Tom was just getting ready to leave for the Dolphin Inn, when his door bell rang. He walked down the stairs to his front door and opened it. Stood outside was a female police officer.

'Mr Derham? Mr Thomas Derham?'

'Yes.'

'I'm Police Constable Harris. I have some rather sad news I'm afraid.'

He looked perplexed.

'You had better come in officer.'

Sat in the lounge Tom waited to hear what she had to say.

'At 4:37 pm your sister Grace was taken to Torbay General hospital. I'm sorry to have to tell you that she passed away shortly afterwards.'

Tom was confused and shocked.

'But I was with her this morning. She was well. I don't understand. Are you sure it is my sister Grace?'

'There is no doubt I'm afraid Mr Derham.'

'Oh dear god,' he whispered in a melancholy confusion.

'I'm so sorry to have to give you such terrible news.'

'What happened? Was it an accident?'

'She had a massive bleed on her brain. A stroke.' She looked at him apologetically and continued,' there was nothing they could do I'm afraid.'

'Grace. Dead. I...I.' He hung his head. The look of confusion now replaced by a despairing sadness. 'Oh dear god. Grace,' he said in another hushed whisper.

PC Harris sat in a respectful silence for a few moments before speaking, 'is there anyone I can call for you? A family friend or neighbour perhaps?'

Momentarily, Tom sat staring expressionlessly at the floor. He let out a sigh.

'No. Thank you. I'll be alright. But that's very kind of you to ask.'

'Not at all. I really am very sorry to bring you such sad news.'

He looked at her. He estimated her to be in her early twenties.

'It's a difficult enough job I expect, but at times like this; it must be very hard.'

She smiled reverently.

'Yes. It can be.'

'Can I make you a cup of tea, or...'

'No I'm fine thank you.'

'Where did it happen?'

'She was on a bus heading to Brixham, when a passenger sat behind her saw her slump forwards...' She paused as she wasn't sure as that what she had said was too much

detail at the present moment. 'I'm sorry, I don't want to…'
He interjected, 'no please. I would like to know.'

PC Harris continued, 'an ambulance was at the scene within four minutes. Your sister was then taken to the hospital.

'Can I ask why the hospital didn't call me?'

'Seemingly, Grace had no identification on her arrival at the hospital. It wasn't until later that the bus company called the hospital to say that they had found her bus pass on the bus. It must have fallen out of her pocket. They contacted us and we contacted one of Grace's neighbours,' she took out her notepad and turned a page and continued, 'a Ms Thompson, who then gave us your address. Ms Thompson told us that as far as she knew, you are the only living relative.' Tom guessed the reason why they had sent an officer rather than phoning him. It was his age. To save her feeling uncomfortable about explaining why they had sent an officer in person he continued, 'thank you for coming to tell me. I appreciate it. It would have been more difficult for me I think, had I just received a phone call.'

She smiled warmly.

'Yes. That's what we thought.'

'Good decision,' he said sincerely.

'Also, we thought that if you wanted to see Grace that it might be easier for you if I took you to the hospital, unless there is someone else that you might want to be there with you?'

He shook his head slowly from side-to-side.

'No. I'll be fine on my own. I'm grateful for the lift. I'm not sure that I'd be up to driving at the moment.'

'I'll arrange a taxi to bring you home afterwards.'
Again he smiled convivially.
'That's very kind of you. I know the police get bad press sometimes. It's a pity people don't see the other side of what you do. Then again, people don't always want to, do they.'
She smiled warmly.
'Would you like to go now. Mr Derham?'
'Tom. You can call me Tom. Yes. I was just about to go out for the evening, so, I'm ready. I'll just get my coat.'

At the hospital, Tom said an emotional goodbye to his sister. They allowed him as much time as he needed to say the words he had to say to her. It was an extremely poignant and moving time for him. Just having welcomed his sister back earlier that morning, with everything seemingly put right, her life was so cruelly taken. Although Tom has a good and positive outlook on life, sometimes, that buoyant optimism was deeply tested.

Over the following few days, his neighbour Claire, had stepped forward and was of great help to him. As he said to her when she'd asked if she was being a nuisance, "Claire you're always there for me, but never in the way." She'd liked that sentiment, it had touched her and would remain with her for the rest of her life.

Chapter Ten

Four days had passed since Grace's death. Tom had been busy making the funeral arrangements. Although she had said to Tom, "don't you ever get fed up with this view," when she last sat on his balcony. In her will she had asked that her ashes be scattered in the river at Mill Pool near Dittisham. That request had come as somewhat of a surprise to Tom. She had loved the river but never really talked about it to him. He thought that there might have been a little jealousy at what Tom had, and she had missed out on due to her late husband. Tom never really got to the bottom of what had actually happened to their relationship and due to her reluctance to talk about it; he never pursued it. He had thought it to be an unhappy marriage.

He was sifting through her effects that he had picked up from her flat. Amongst them was a shoe box of paperwork. For the most part it consisted of the usual items: bank statements, old bills, a few treasured birthday and Christmas cards, a couple of letters and an address book; then he came to a large brown envelope. He opened it and a few photographs fell out onto his table top. He turned his head to look at one of them, and an unexpected realisation of what he was looking at became clear to him. They were photographs of Grace's husband with other women. As he picked up each one in turn, they became a little more explicit. Not erotic, but lots of kissing and sexual fondling. He sat back in his sofa. Grace had *never* talked to Tom about it. She had suffered his adulterous behaviour alone and in silence. He knew her late husband could turn quite nasty with her, and although Grace had always denied it, he had a suspicion that he had physically hurt her on occasions. He had also "invested" Grace's own savings in his failed and sometimes dodgy business ventures and lost it all. She'd had an unfair and difficult life with him. This saddened him deeply. She hadn't deserved that. Had he known, he could have helped her. It was little wonder why Grace was like she was with him sometimes; sarcastic and short tempered. The animosity towards Tom at times, was her only release from her nightmare.

He looked up from the photographs and out over the river. 'Why didn't you talk to me Grace?' he said in a low whisper, 'if only you would have talked to me.'

After a few moments he continued to go through the rest of her effects. Eventually he came to a news paper clipping. It was the report of her husband's death due to a climbing accident. He had apparently been quite a competent climber and there had been a Coroner's Inquest, whose conclusion was "Accidental Death". Then, something occurred to him. In a deep concentration, he spread out her effects across the table. He picked up a drawing and a sheet of paper which contained a Google search print out. He hadn't seen the connection when he saw them the first time. He'd dismissed them as being unimportant. Now he looked at the two items through very different eyes. Then, a sudden and shocking realisation shook him to the core. 'Oh sweet *Jesus* Grace. What did you *do*?'

The Google article was about climbing accidents through equipment failure. The drawing he was looking at was a sketch of a climbing harness, but it had been altered in such a way that it would fail. It was so subtle that an arrogant overconfident climber could miss…and did!

A cold steel like chill ran through his body that made him physically judder.

'Oh Grace. Dear god Grace.'

He sat back in his chair in the knowledge of what she had done. Of that, there was little doubt in his mind. He sat in a stunned silence…

His phone ringing shocked him back. He looked down at his phone. It was Lottie. He didn't know whether he was in the right frame of mind to answer; his mind was in a spiral, but all the same, he picked it up and answered.

'Hi Tom. I thought I'd give you a call and see how things are?' Of course Tom had yet to tell Lottie about Grace.

'Hello. Are you there Tom?' She said jovially.

'Hello Lottie. How nice to hear from you. Sorry about the delay. I've had a bit of a time of it recently, and my mind is all over the map at the moment I'm afraid.'

'Oh. I'm really sorry to hear that Tom. Is there anything I can do to help?'

He didn't know what to say to her. He looked down at the table and the drawing.

'Tom. Are you alright Tom?' she said with an earnest concern.

'Yes. Sorry Lottie. The thing is…Grace died a few days ago, unexpectedly. A stroke.'

'Oh god Tom. I'm so *so* sorry to hear that. How awful for you.'

'Yes. It was quite a shock.' He looked once more at the drawing on the table.

'Do you want me to call round?'

'No. I'm fine thanks.'

'I don't mind Tom. I really don't.'

She left him in silence fleetingly, allowing him a little time to think.

'Actually, yes I'd like that I think.'

'OK. Do you want me to pick anything up for you on the way?'

'No. I've everything I need. In fact, thinking about it. It'd be good if I got out of the house for a while. How about a walk somewhere? I could come over to you?'

'No. I wouldn't hear of it.'

'Actually Lottie I'd quite like a drive. Could I meet you in Brixham perhaps? Would that be alright? I have to call into the estate agent to give them the instructions for the sale of Grace's flat. I had said I would go tomorrow, but…'

'Yes. That's *absolutely* fine with me Tom. What time and where?'

'Shall we say One O'clock?'

'That's cool for me. Where?'

'Do you know the pedestrian walkway to the Marina?'

'By the harbour?'

'Yes. I'll meet you on one of the benches along the harbour wall. Is that alright?'

'Of course it is. I'll see you there Tom.'

'OK. Bye for now Lottie.'

'Bye Tom.'

He put his phone down on the table and sat back once again into his sofa. He stared at Grace's drawing, the coroner's report in the news clipping and the adulterous photographs. He gathered them together, walked out of his lounge, up the stairs and on into his study. By his desk was a shredder. He picked it up and placed it on his desk. First in was the news clipping, next Grace's drawing. Then he paused, held up the photographs and said in a low, but meaningful tone, 'you swine.' and proceeded to shred. When it had gone silent, he stared down at the shredder and then out through his window and across the river.

'Now you can rest in peace Grace. May you sleep deeply and troubled free.' For the first time since hearing the news of the death of his sister, he hadn't shed a tear or even allowed himself to grieve. Now, sat there in his study at his desk, he mourned her passing, and also that finally, she was at peace. A solitary tear appeared and fell from his left eye onto his desk. His conscience did prick him however; he knew that what he had just done was wrong, but he concluded that it would serve no purpose to inform anyone now. What was done…was done and that would be the end of it. He would never disclose or discuss what he had discovered; with anyone. He did however, wonder why Grace had not destroyed the evidence. He assumed that in all probability, Grace *did* want someone to find it after she had gone. He surmised that, for her, it would serve as a kind of atonement. He turned around, closed the door and left his study to its secret.

Chapter Eleven

Tom had been to the estate agent to arrange for Grace's flat to be put on the market. With the knowledge that young people of the area really struggle to remain in the place that they were born due to properties being owned by people living outside the area and the houses and apartments used as holiday homes and lets, meant that the price range and availability was beyond their reach. He had always thought it unfair. With this in mind, and against the better judgment of the estate agent's advice, he set the price of her house, below that of the market value and a caveat, that only a local could purchase it. It is a nice flat with a harbour view. A young couple starting out in life, would be given an opportunity to continue to work and live in the place they were born.

He walked along the pedestrianised promenade which follows the harbour wall looking to see where Lottie was sat. A little earlier, she had text him to say that she had arrived in Brixham. A short distance further on, and just past the little wooden café cabin, he saw her. She waved. He walked over to her; she stood up and hugged him.

'I'm so sorry Tom.'

He held her for a few moments and then released himself as he felt quite emotional and wanted to keep his feelings in check.

He smiled.

'Thank you Lottie.'

They both sat down on the bench. She looked at him questioningly.

'It was sudden and catastrophic. There was nothing they could have done. I was with her that morning. She had changed.'

'Changed?'

'I went for a walk earlier that morning and decided to go and visit Daisy. As I hadn't planned it, and I usually buy some flowers for her, I'd picked a few wild woodland flowers. I'd tied them together into a small bunch by using a few long pieces of dried ornamental grass that was lying on the ground. When I got to the cemetery, Grace was standing there by Daisy's graveside. I was…I don't know, startled I guess.

Apparently, she visited Daisy whenever she could. I'd no idea she did that. We sat down together on one of the benches and chatted for a while. She was different. When I just said to you that she had changed, she told me that she'd had a kind of epiphany; in which she realised how she had been with me over the past few years. She said she was sorry for the way she had been quite foul with me sometimes and treated me unfairly. It was quite a moment for her...and me. Sadly, and ironically, having had this epiphany and wanting to build bridges...within a few hours she was dead.' He paused briefly and reflectively before continuing,' you see, it's that randomness of death Lottie. Life lulls you into the illusion that it will go on forever and that you have enough time to carry on being the way you are, putting things off until a later date, until it's too late. Each day Lottie...make each day count.'

'I don't have any words Tom.'

He looked at her.

'Maybe you don't Lottie, but out of respect, I at least expected a beard.'

Her eyes widened and she didn't quite know how to respond. Then Tom smiled and winked. She nodded her head in the knowledge that Tom survived this life by having a good sense of humour, and never taking himself too seriously. It's a good way to look at life she thought to herself.

'What is it with this beard fixation?'

He laughed.

'Yes, quite right. I'll drop the beard thing now. I'll never mention it again.'

'Yes you will.'

He nodded his head.

'I know.' He paused fleetingly before continuing, 'the funeral is next Tuesday. You're welcome to come Lottie.'

She sat quietly for a few moments before answering, 'that's very kind Tom, but I think that it's an occasion for those that knew Grace to share together.'

He respected her sentiment.

'Will she be buried near Daisy?'

'No. She left instructions to be cremated and her ashes scattered in the Dart at Mill Pool near Dittisham.'

'I see.'

'The skipper of the Carlina very kindly offered to take me and…Grace, there. But I'd like to take her on one last sail.' He paused momentarily again and continued, 'I understand why you wouldn't want to come to the funeral, and you might think this a little odd, but you could come with me if you like, to Mill Pool. I think perversely, she'd like that.'

'No Tom. I think you should go on your own.'

'OK. I understand Lottie. If you change your mind, let me know. I wouldn't at all mind.'

For a few moments they sat in silence as a deep sea trawler made its way into the inner-harbour after possibly spending days at sea. A small group of children were excitedly crabbing nearby; their lines dangling over the harbour wall into the sea, and a solitary seagull sat patiently on the wall near them, its bright yellow eyes fixed on the crab line in the hope of a fresh, tasty, crab morsel. Lottie broke the contemplation, 'did you ever come here with Daisy Tom?'

He smiled.

'Yes. Many times. As you know her absolute favourite was Warfleet, but I think sometimes she missed the company, or buzz if you like, of other children. She had no inhibitions and would just go right over to inspect the other's buckets to see if the crabs were any bigger than hers. Yes. She liked it here.'

'I nearly forgot?'

'What?'

'The reason I phoned you this morning,' she paused a moment as she thought that it might not be an appropriate time, but Tom interjected, 'and..?'

'And what?'

'You were going to say why you phoned me?'

'Oh. Erm. Look if this isn't an appropriate time, just tell me.'

'Make each day count Lottie.'

She smiled.

'I have been thinking about, you know, your jigsaw puzzle. I'd like to start on it. How do you feel about that?'

'You mean you haven't sorted it out yet. You've had days.'

She laughed.

'Yeah, well. It might help if I had a little bit of information, you know; save me having to guess.'

'OK. I'll let you off. You have another day.'

'Yeah…right.'

'What do you need to know?'

'Well I know your surname so that's a start.'

Tom thought how did she possibly know his surname; he couldn't remember giving it to her. Then it occurred to him; it's engraved on Daisy's headstone.

He nodded his head.

'Yes. Derham.'

'It's a nice name.'

'I had no choice.'

'I know.'

'You really don't mind doing this?'

'No. I love history and doing this is just another form of researching, albeit a family history. If I sketch a landscape for instance, I like to get the background of the place. Gives it a context. It's how *I* do things anyway.'

She took out a small note pad from her bag.

Tom smiled at her.

'What?'

'I thought that you'd have something a little more, you know, hi tech.'

'Like what for example?'

'Well, for jotting down notes and things; ipad, or something like that.'

'And you have one I suppose?'

'I do.'

She narrowed her eyes.

'You don't do you.'

'No.'

'I like my little note pad, I make preliminary sketches in it. I've got one of you actually.'

'Of me?'

'Yes.'

'Can I see it?'

'No.'

'No?'

'When it's done and I'm cool with it. Then I'll show it to you.'

'You're a bit bossy really aren't you.'

She set off laughing.

Tom looked at her. He really enjoyed being in her company. It made him feel good about himself. He was just wondering if he should tell her so, when…

'If it's not inappropriate to say Tom; I do like being around you. It lights up my little day.'

'Well. I wish I could say the same.'

She looked at him with a slight hesitancy before they both set off laughing.

'I was just thinking,' he said, 'did you come in your car?'

'Nope. Bus.'

'Each time we meet I seem to ask you this but, have you anything planned for the rest of the afternoon?'

'Well I was going to do my nails.'

'Oh…OK.'

She laughed.

'I was kidding. Why do you have something more interesting than nails to offer?'

'Well, I do like Brixham, but with you mentioning just then, about history, a thought occurred to me.'

'You're a quick thinker.'

'Yes. It comes over me like that sometimes. Quite randomly. Have you heard of Torcross?'

'Yes.'

'Have you ever been to Torcross?'

'No.'

'Would you like to go to Torcross?'

'Yes.'

'Well then.'

'Isn't it near a beach?'

'Yes, Slapton Sands?'

'Well, I'm good to go. You mentioned the history thing. Did something happen there?'

'Oh yes, something rather extraordinary occurred there. But I thought it might just be a nice place to sit and give you a few more details that might help you to find the correct picture.'

She gave him a broad smile.

'Well, let's go.'

Chapter Twelve

A tank, a sunken village and crab baguettes

The drive to Torcross is a pleasant one; the road passing as it does through some very pretty Devonshire countryside and villages. The road in places, narrowing to the width of a single car, such as Stoke Fleming and the village they were just approaching, Strete.

'Oh my days. This is tricky driving Tom. It's a good job you've got a Mini.'
'Hmm. Each time I come here, I can't imagine how tanks and other military vehicles got through here.'
'Tanks?'
'Yep. American tanks. I'll explain when we get to Torcross.'

'It's a beautiful drive though Tom.'

Further on as they drove up a steep incline the road meandered slightly to the left. Through the gaps in the trees, Lottie spotted an almost perfect semi-circular bay with a crescent formed beach at the shoreline.
'*Wow*! *That's* impressive.'
Without taking his eyes of the road Tom replied, 'it's Blackpool Sands.'
'Blackpool?'
'Not that Blackpool, obviously,' he replied with just a hint of sarcasm.
They had driven past the sign saying, Blackpool Sands, but Lottie had not seen it.
'It looks gorgeous.'
'It's gorgeous, and very popular.'
'I bet.'

A mile or so on, and Lottie glimpsed her first view of Slapton Sands.
'Is that Slapton?'
'Yes.'
'It looks *amazing*. The beach seems to go on forever. What's on the other side of the road? It looks like a lake.'
'It's Slapton Ley. A fresh water nature reserve. It's quite a unique landscape. The road is built on a shingle spit; on one side is the sea and on the other, the Ley which is fresh water. Occasionally in the past, when there's been a combination of low pressure, storms and a spring tide, parts of the road have been washed away.

Unfortunately, possibly due in part to climate change, two of the consequences of that being sea level rise and more extreme weather events, it does appear that it will happen with more frequency in the future. You'll see when we drop down onto the straight stretch that runs to Torcross, there's a kind of dog leg where the road's been breached and has had to be moved in land a little. There is talk that if it happens again, it'll be left to be reclaimed by the sea. It will effectively sever the journey from Dartmouth to Torcross and the fresh water nature reserve and its wildlife, will be lost for ever. It would be so very sad and have a huge environmental impact on this exceptional landscape.'

'Can't they just keep repairing it?'

'They say it's too costly.'

'Couldn't they take some money from the defence budget or somewhere else?' she said cynically.

Tom laughed and shook his head slowly from side to side.

The road began its steep descent down through a series of sharp bends to Strete Gate where the road, with the exception of that small deviation, follows an almost straight run of over a mile or so, to Torcross village.

'This is wonderful,' she said. 'Why have I never been here before.'

Just a little before the village, they came to the car park. They found a space easily enough, parked up and got out of the car. Tom went to get a ticket. He returned, placed it on his windscreen and closed the door.

'Come and look at this.'

'Oh yes,' she said suggestively.

He smiled wryly.

He walked her over to the end of the car park where on top of a mounded cobbled area, sits a WWII American Sherman tank. Lottie read the inscription and turned to Tom. She gave him an enquiring look.

'Let's find somewhere to sit and I'll tell you what happened here. I'll try not to bore you.'

'You could never do that.'

'Oh yes I could.'

She laughed and linked his arm which now had become the norm to which neither of them gave it a second thought. They crossed the road, and on to the concrete pathway behind the sea wall. Lottie looked over the wall and out across the panorama.

'It's *Stunning* Tom. And such *big* skies. I bet there isn't a sky so full of stars as there is here at night. I'd *love* to see that.'

'I have never really thought about that; but yes I can imagine so, on a clear night. We can come back and sit on the beach if you like; there's something I want to show you first.'

'I feel a history lesson coming on.'

He smiled broadly and nodded his head.

They followed the path along the sea wall, passing a café, a pub, several terraced houses, and a scattering of detached properties and a Tea Room, all of which having glorious, uninterrupted sea views. At the end of the path is a large and rather dominant property that are now holiday apartments. He turned right, then next left and together they began to walk up the hill. A little way up, he took a left turn. In front of them was a gradient of steep steps, the end of which couldn't be seen from street level. He led the way; she followed closely behind. At the top, on their right hand side, there was two detached houses, he stopped a few steps beyond, turned and pointed.

'How about that for a view.'

The panoramic view looked out across the whole of the bay, Slapton Sands, and the long straight road separating the salty sea water from the sweet fresh water of Slapton Ley nature reserve.

'This is extraordinary Tom. What a view.' She took out her phone and took a few pictures. He sat on a low dry stone wall and let her absorb the scene for a few minutes in silence.

She looked at him.

'So, what happened here then? It's something to do with the tank isn't it?'

He gave her a warm smile.

'During the Second World War the US 4th Division was stationed here. The Division was to take part in the joint operation known as Overlord. You might know it better as the D-Day landings,' she acknowledged it with a nod of her head, he continued, 'the Normandy landing sites were given code names; this Division was to land on

Utah Beach. In preparation, a rehearsal for the landing took place here at Slapton Sands. On the night of the 27th April 1944, the flotilla was out at sea in Lyme Bay,' he pointed out to sea, 'just out there, waiting for the order to begin their landing on the beach at daybreak. This was given the name Exercise Tiger. All seemed to be going to plan, when abruptly, all hell was let loose. Explosions, guns firing, shouting, screams of anguish, fire, ships sinking. Then an eerie silence fell before the moans and cries for help filled the night air.

In the weeks that followed, every enquiry about that night hit a solid wall of silence. As soon as the wounded were able enough, they were separated and moved further and further west to other hospitals, some as far as Wales. When they were fit enough to return to duty, they were dispersed to different Divisions and Units. They were told not to discuss, or even mention, what had happened that night; that if they did, they would be arrested and court marshalled.

Right up until a few years ago, it had consistently been denied by the UK and American governments that anything happened here. However, eventually through the insistence and heroic questioning, by a couple of locals, of both the US and UK governments, they eventually admitted what had happened. The truth finally surfaced, and the relatives of those young lads who died here that night, finally knew what had really happened to their: husband, son, brother, uncle, father.

That night several German E Boats, which carried torpedoes, had chanced upon the fleet of ships and started to strafe them with machine gunfire and the torpedoes. Because the British Admiralty was using a different radio frequency than the US, when the explosions started, no one knew what was happening; they thought perhaps it was part of the exercise. When they realised that they were under attack, they tried to raise the British Naval ships that had been escorting them to ask for immediate assistance, but couldn't because of the lack of communication between the Brits and US due to the two different frequencies.

The sad, and tragic irony is that, by the morning of the 28th April 1944, out in that bay 946 - some say as many as 1200 - young American boys had lost their lives. On Utah Beach in Normandy on the morning of the actual D-Day landings…197 were killed.'

Lottie looked intensely at Tom, and then out to sea and Lyme Bay.

'What a horrible, horrible thing to do to those relatives and loved ones. Lead them to believe that they had died in action in France…I guess that's what they told them?'

Tom nodded.

'I suppose at the time, they couldn't afford morale to be flattened by such a tragic and avoidable event. But I agree, to know the truth and suppress it for so long afterwards, is both a disgrace and so very sad. I wasn't born in Devon. I moved here in nineteen-seventy-two. I was born in Shropshire. My parents used to come to Devon for their holidays. This was one of the places they brought me to. It looked very different then. There was no sea wall or any of the sea defences on the beach.

I remember as a young boy seeing signs on the beach warning of the possibility of finding live ammunition. After all those years, some of that history was still coming to the surface. Of course, it was exciting to me as a boy, I didn't really understand or think about the significance of it then. I didn't really know that much about the war, as people who had lived through it, wanted to forget about it and move on to a better World. Being here as a boy, I would just eagerly sift through the small pebbles hoping to find a bullet or two…or whatever.'

'You just said that there were no sea defences then? Why do they need them now? Is it because of climate change and sea level rise that you mentioned before?'

'Yes, and no.' He gave her a cheeky schoolboy grin and continued,' you surely don't want another history lesson do you?'

She threw her head back and let out a hearty laugh.

'Well hell yeah!'

'Well, actually, strictly speaking it's a bit of that, but also with a little geology thrown in the mix.'

She smiled and nodded.

'Cool.'

'Then walk this way mademoiselle.'

They retraced their steps back a few paces and then at the side of the house, turned left through a narrow gap between the two houses. After a few more paces, they came to a low fence; to their right, steep descending steps leading to a cove; at the back of which are a few fairly new houses which serve as beachfront accommodation.

'Very nice,' said Lottie.

'Good spot eh. And your own beach.'

'So?'

'Oh yes. Torcross and Slapton Sands never used to have artificial sea defences, because it had its own natural defences.' He pointed to a rocky platform that ran at the back of the foreshore above the high tide mark. He continued, 'you see that flattish, rocky outcrop there?'

'Yep.'

On that platform used to sit the village of Hallsands. It had been a fishing community for generations. On the twenty-sixth of January 1917 the village was swept out to sea. A massive storm slammed into the coast here and along the entire length of Slapton Sands. Historically, they'd had severe storms and the village and the houses here and along Torcross had always survived. However, something quite significant had changed. Out in the bay, over millennia, the undulating shape of the sea bed had created huge gravel ridges through the ebb and flow of the tide. These gravel banks were the natural defence for this part of the coastline. As the storm surges came towards the shore, the gravel dispersed the energy of the waves and the impact on the coast was greatly reduced. However, the decision at the time, to dredge and remove the shingle to expand a naval dockyard at Keyham, thirty miles away, led three years later to the small harbour sea wall being swept away; the beach level dropping between seven and twelve feet, and thereby greatly reducing the natural defences to the sea's energy. This incompetence and short-sightedness left this part of the coastline vulnerable. Hallsands was the price, as was having to spend millions of pounds on erecting sea defences and constantly having to repair the main road that we just came down into Torcross.'

She let out a sigh.

'Wow. What a thing. You seem to know an *awful* lot about this stuff.'

'It's a bit of a thing with me. I studied geology and engineering.'

'Ahh. That'll be it then,' she said with a cheeky grin.

'Oh I could talk for hours about Longshore drift.'

'Please don't feel you have to…interesting as it is, I'm sure.'

He started laughing.

'You only need to ask.'

'I'll bear that in mind. It is fascinating though, and scary, just how so easily we can upset the balance of nature.'

'If, or when, that road eventually goes. The whole, morphology, or shape if you like, of this area will change.'

'How?'

'Come on; one last thing.'

She smiled and followed him back to the dry stone wall overlooking the bay and lagoon.

'As I said the road separates the salt water from the fresh water. Not only will wildlife, plant life and fish be affected, the whole landscape will be changed. The sea will flow in and replace the fresh water lagoon all the way back to the road over there,' he pointed to the Kingsbridge road, 'therefore making it into a large open bay.'

She looked intensely at the lagoon.

'Oh yeah! I see what you mean. The whole scene will be totally different.'

'Unrecognisable to how it had been before.'

'What do you think will happen to all the houses and the Tea Room, café and pub?'

'Well, the way I see it is that, there are not only residents here, there is an extended seasonal business and tourist industry. It may be small scale, but it contributes towards the economy of this area. They need and depend on it. So, you know where we crossed the road from the car park where the seawall starts?'

She pointed, 'over there?'

'Yes. I think they'll construct a harbour wall there and that would protect the houses and businesses. That's what I would do anyway.'

'Yeah, I can see that. But, how are the tourists and locals going to get here with no road?'

'They will have to come from Kingsbridge. They will shore up the road over there with a sea wall and defences, as they have done here at Torcross.' He paused a moment and then continued,' a more radical idea: a ferry could run from the newly constructed Torcross harbour to Strete Gate at the bottom of the Dartmouth road. There's a large enough car park there to accommodate the volume of traffic.' He shrugged his shoulders, 'Just my observation anyway.'

She looked again at the landscape and then smiling looked at Tom.

'You're a proper smarty aren't you.'

He grinned.

'I have my occasional flashes of brilliance.'

'Doesn't it make you tired all this theorising?'

'No. But it does make me hungry.'

'*Oh*. Do you fancy…' he interjected, 'I'll tell you what I fancy Lottie.'

'Oh yeah,' she said suggestively.

He smiled and shook his head slowly from side to side.

'A cream tea and a strong coffee.'

'Now that *is* good idea.'

At the Sea Breeze Tea Room, having eaten their cream teas; Tom had finished off his coffee and Lottie a glass of chilled Chardonnay; they walked across the pathway and stepped through the gap in the sea wall and made their way to some flat rocks on the beach at the foot of the cliff and sat down.

'I must try to stop letting you keep buying the food and drinks.'

'Well, old habits are hard to let go I guess. These things take time.'

She punched him playfully in the arm. Tom though, wasn't convinced, and thought that she might have been aiming for his chin. He held his hands up in the air in submission.

'OK OK.'

She narrowed her eyes and then set off laughing.

'Oh yeah laughter…that's good,' he said with a hint of cynicism.

Her expression changed.

'Tom. Let's talk about you.'

'Me?'

She nodded knowingly.

'Yes Tom, you.'

'Ahh.'

'Do you still want to find out what happened to Hellene?'

His demeanour became more reflective.

'That's why I asked you here Lottie. It's a good place to contemplate thoughts, but, as I've said to you before, I really don't know what more there is to discover.

As I told you at Warfleet Creek, I tried everything and searched everywhere. There is nothing new to find.'

'That's not what I asked Tom. If you want me to try. I would like to do this for you. I might, as you say, draw a blank. But…I'd like to try to help you if I can. Let me do that for you Tom.'

He looked at her and sensed her genuine honesty in wanting to resolve what has been, since that time of her leaving, a World of shadows and silhouettes.

'If you think that you can discover something that might help me to give some understanding as to why she left; that would be really welcomed and appreciated. But I don't want to put you out Lottie. You have your own life to live.'

'And to choose *how* to live your life is important, isn't it Tom?'

He smiled.

'Yes.'

'Well then.'

Again he smiled.

'What do you need to know?'

'The date she left, her maiden name and any information in the letter – that wouldn't be too painful to you, for me to read, and anything at all that happened afterwards.'

Tom sat back and gave great thought to what he would tell her next. He disclosed the contents of the letter, dates, and all the information relating to names and locations of any relatives and friends of Hellene that he could recall. Lottie was focused on every word he spoke as she jotted down the information in her note pad. Tom looked at her apologetically.

'Having just gone through it all again, I really don't think that there is anything new there Lottie.'

She smiled.

'A book may be finished; but you can always add another page or two.'

He returned a warm smile.

'I've one more thing to show you.'

'Oh yeah,' she said once again enticingly.

'Stop it you.'

She feigned surprise.

'What?'

'You know very well what.'

'Okay. What is it then?' she said beaming a smile.

She followed him back across the path, and down the side of the Sea Breeze Tea Room. This took them to the main road. They crossed it which brought them to a small viewing area of the Ley. They sat down on a bench with a view through wild grasses and reeds and out and across the stillness of the water. There were all kinds of wildfowl, and birdsong and the flora was in absolute contrast with the seaward side.

'This is *so* beautiful Tom. It's so tranquil and peaceful. You wouldn't believe that this could be the same place as the beach over there.'

'This is what will be lost, if and when the road goes. I wanted you to see it close up.'

They sat together in silence for a short time and watched as a young boy and girl fed bread crumbs to a bevy of Swans; the children watched over lovingly by their mum and dad. An innocent pastime, from which a life-long memory was being made.

After a few more minutes, they left and crossed the road to the sands. They walked along the path to the Start Bay Inn. She looked at Tom.

'Tempting.'

'I'm driving Lottie. But, I suppose a small white wine would be OK.'

'I'll get these. I'm just having a fruit juice.'

Tom's eyes widened. In contrast, her eyes became narrower. She stared at him, 'don't you dare.'

He grinned.

Tom sat at one of the tables and took in the view while Lottie went inside to get the drinks.

Within a few minutes Lottie returned; she was carrying the two glasses. She placed them on the table and slipped a ticket underneath the ashtray. Tom looked at the ticket and then questioningly to Lottie.

'I hope you like fresh crab?'

'I do, but...'

'Bought us a baguette each. I saw a bloke eating one in there and I couldn't resist.'

He smiled.

'Well OK then.'

'Just trying to kick the habit…you know. Letting you persuade me that you'll pay every time we eat.'
Tom nodded.
'Hmm.'
'Thanks for today Tom. Yet again, you have made my little World feel that much bigger.'
Tom liked that sentiment.
'Thank you for listening to my historical and geological ramblings, however fascinating they may be.'
She laughed.
'You're very modest. And I mean that in an honest way. You really are a very humble man. Do you know how rare that is in a bloke?'
He smirked.
'Not sure about that Lottie…really.'
'You just proved the point.'
A voice came from behind, 'she's right you know.' It came from a woman sat by herself at a table.
'Sorry?' said Tom.
'Blokes and modesty. They don't always arrive together.' She pointed to a man out in the bay who was whizzing quite dangerously near to the edge of the beach on a jet ski where children were swimming. She continued, 'that's my fella. Totally uncontaminated by any sense of modesty. A right big head.' She raised a glass to her lips and in one, emptied the remnants; she then picked up a wine bottle and refilled her glass to the rim. She raised it to Tom and Lottie and said, 'prick!' then slumped back into her chair. Lottie tried to contain her self from laughing by clamping her lips tightly

together. She wasn't successful however, and little uncontrollable spurts of air and squeals were emitted from her mouth. Tom was also struggling to not laugh. Luckily, the waitress calling out their number, side-tracked them.

'Yes here,' said Lottie waving the ticket. The waitress placed the two baguettes and salad down on the table top.

The waitress gave them both an easy smile.

'Enjoy.'

They replied together, 'thank you.'

They soon polished off their food and decided it was time to leave Torcross.

They headed back to Dartmouth. At the ferry they said their goodbyes, with Lottie promising that she would be in touch with any news she'd found for Tom.

Lottie had said to Tom, "a book may be finished; but you can always add another page or two." Those added pages to Tom's story however, would completely alter the storyline of *his* book, and as a consequence, change the course of his life…

Chapter Thirteen

The weather had turned on the day of Grace's funeral. A torrent of rain washed down the road towards the river, as those that had come to pay their respects filled the the pews at the little church of St Thomas of Canterbury in Kingswear. Grace had requested that the service be held there in her Will.

Tom was pleasantly surprised at the number of people that had turned up to say their farewells.

After the service Tom stood in the vestibule to thank those that had come as they left the church. As with many funerals, there are those that attend that no one seems to recognise. Grace's funereal was no exception. There were a few people that he was certain he had never met before that day. They could of course be friends that he'd not been introduced to, or old friends from her distant past or work colleagues.

And occasionally at such processions, illegitimate children have come to the surface. Strange occurrences and revelations can, and do happen at funerals.

The rain had stopped and the sun began to break through the clouds. Tom had decided that his house would be difficult for many to get to with restricted parking and the steep climb up the hill or steps. So, he had hired a room at the Ship Inn which sits adjacent to the church to hold the commemorative meal. The vicar had made the announcement about the meal at the end of the service; that all would be welcome. Looking at the numbers, Tom was glad that he had taken that decision. A buffet would be laid on, and now that the inclement weather had improved, the food could be eaten outside in the beer garden which has views across the Dart.

After that short period where everyone approaches the next of kin to pay their respects with their various eulogies and sentiments; the time of consumption begins. Generally, a simpler and more relaxed atmosphere settles over the funeral-goers. It was at this point however, outside in the beer garden, where a man that Tom had noticed earlier, who seemed to be a little *too* pre-occupied with glancing over at him, which had made him feel strangely uncomfortable - walked over to him. He put out his hand.
'I'm very sorry for your loss.'

Tom acknowledged the man's sentiment with a graceful nod of the head.

'Thank you.'

'I'm Greg.'

'Ahh. Well, thank you for coming today Greg, I'm sure Grace would have been pleased.'

The man looked at Tom with a fixed, unemotional detachment.

'I was a friend of Lawrence. That's how I knew Grace.'

A chill ran down Tom's spine. Lawrence was Grace's husband.

'I see.'

'Yes. I was his climbing partner the day he fell.' A more intense, piercing look followed.

Tom had to show that he had no knowledge of what he had stumbled across; the probability of what had really occurred that day. He could give nothing away in his expression.

'Yes. It was a *terrible* accident,' he said with deep sincerity, 'Grace was absolutely devastated.'

Once again the emotional detachment from Greg.

'Yes. It was as you say, a terrible accident. Strange though.'

'Strange; how?'

'Lawrence was such an accomplished climber; even now it's hard to believe that he would miss that vital piece of equipment.'

Tom nodded his head reverently slowly up and down.

'As the coroner said, it was a most unfortunate accident. People can, and do, make the most fundamental mistakes, which can be costly.'

Greg looked penetratingly into Tom's eyes. Tom could sense that he suspected something more than a "fundamental mistake" had transpired that day. Tom also knew that any evidence pointing to that…no longer existed.

Once again Greg put out his hand.

'It's been nice meeting you. Once again, I am sorry for your loss.'

Tom smiled convivially and shook his hand.

'Thank you for coming. As I said, Grace would be pleased that you took the time to come and say a final farewell to her.' Tom had to hold his hospitable expression; inside he was cringing. Greg was probably one of the *last* people that Grace would want to be there. Greg turned and walked out of the beer garden, and out of Tom and Grace's life forever. Tom guessed that he had come to the funeral with the expectation that he might possibly find an answer; that expectation wasn't met and he'd left with nothing; only the suspicions he came with; suspicions that could never be proven now, or at any time in the future.

The rest of the day went very well. Tom touched base with many of Grace's friends and colleagues whom were previously unknown to him. He listened to them with great interest and happiness on hearing how, previously unknown to him, Grace had touched so many lives. He learned so much more about his sister that day, for which he would be ever grateful. Funerals can sometimes help to add to the whole picture of the deceased's life. Memories that have not been shared to the next of kin can help to inform and fill in the missing spaces. It is a joy, yet also a sadness, that such reminiscences, recollections and heartfelt sentiments, are discovered and said, too late.

All in all, Grace had a good "send off". As Tom had been at the service, Grace would have been equally surprised; not so much at the number of people that turned up in the most inclement of weather, but of what was said about her. Although an agnostic himself, Tom knew that Grace was religious. He hoped that her God had allowed her to hear the many kindnesses said that day at her final farewell.

Chapter Fourteen

Tom was in the supermarket buying a few provisions when his phone rang. He placed his basket on the floor and took out his phone; it was Lottie.

'Hello Lottie. How are you?'

'Hi Tom. I'm good thanks. I just wanted to ask how it went yesterday?'

'Look, I'm in the supermarket at the moment, can I phone you back in about half an hour or so?'

'Yeah, if that's OK with you?

'That'll be great.'

'Cool. We'll speak later then. Bye Tom.'

'Bye Lottie.'

Back on his balcony he returned Lottie's call.

'Hi Lottie. Sorry about that, you caught me with my hands full.'

'That's alright Tom thanks for getting back to me. I've called for two reasons really: to ask how it went yesterday and secondly, that I think I *have* found something.'

'You've found something?'

'Yes. Regarding Hellene.'

'Really. You *have*?'

'Yes, I *think* so.

He let out a sigh.

'Are you OK Tom?'

'Yes. It's just...you know.'

'I'm sorry Tom, I should have been more sensitive. You have only just said goodbye to Grace. I should have been more aware of that...talking about Hellene in that way. It's such bad timing.'

'No no Lottie. I didn't mean for it to come across like that about the timing. It's, well, with all that's happened, I'm not sure how I feel about going any further with trying to find answers to that part of my life. Maybe I should just let it go.'

There was a momentary silence.

'Are you still there Lottie?'

'Yes...yes I'm here. There is a third reason why I called.'

'What is it?'

'If the offer for me to come with you to scatter Grace's ashes is still open. I would like to go with you.'

Tom didn't need to think about his reply.

'That would be lovely Lottie. I told you that the skipper of the Carlina had very kindly offered to take me, and that I'd said I wanted to do it on my own.'

'Yes, I remember Tom.'

'I don't want to be on my own Lottie. So, yes please, if you're sure you don't mind?'

'I absolutely don't mind.'

'About the other reason you called. Let me have a think about it. It maybe that Grace's death is still a little raw and that I just want the clouds to lift a little. We'll talk about it when we meet up if that's alright?'

'That's totally alright. I understand Tom.'

'You're a good soul Lottie. Do you know that.'

She laughed.

'Well that's a first. I've been called many things, but never a good soul.'

'Well there you go.'

Once again she let out an honest and sincere laugh.

'The crematorium is going to give me a call when Grace's ashes are ready to be picked up. I'll let you know when I hear from them.'

'OK Tom.'

'So, what are you up to today?'

'Well, I've gone and got myself a commission.'

'That's *fabulous!* That's really great Lottie.'

'Nothing major and it's not for a celebrity or nobility or anything; but it'll keep me in food, petrol and wine for a while…and not in that particularly order.'

Tom laughed.

'Well done you.'

'What are you up to Tom?'

'I'm going to pick up Butterfly's outboard. A friend has repaired it for me. It wasn't anything major; it just needed a bit of TLC.'

She laughed again.

'Don't we all. Right, well, I'd better get back to my easel.'

'OK Lottie. As I say, I'll give you a call, and I'll have a think about, you know…'

'Alright. Cool. See you soon Tom. Take care.'

'You too Lottie. Bye for now.'

Tom had said that he really didn't know how he felt at that moment about any revelation to do with Hellene's disappearance. Although, he was intrigued to discover what Lottie thinks she might have found. However, a coffee or two later, and he'd had a change of heart. He had decided to proceed with the journey; to see where it would take him, and where it would ultimately end…

A view from the balcony

Chapter Fifteen

Early June

Tom and Butterfly, were waiting at the small pontoon where the Dartmouth-Dittisham ferry pulls in. He was only allowed a limited time to tie up and wait there for Lottie. So as soon as she was about to leave for Kingswear, she'd called him. He in turn, had then set off to collect Butterfly.

A few days earlier, having picked up Grace's ashes and received permission from the Harbourmaster to scatter them in the river, he'd contacted Lottie with the day and time. He had also told her that he had thought everything through, and had decided to let her carry on with her search. After she had left him the last time they met, she had asked him if she could have a copy of the letter sent by Hellene to him. He had agreed and scanned it over to her.

Within five minutes or so of Tom tying up, Lottie appeared at the top of the steps. She waved animatedly, and then realised that it was quite a solemn occasion and lowered her arms. Tom smiled acquiescently. She walked down the steps to the pontoon.

'Hi Tom.'

He helped her into the boat.

'Hello Lottie. How are you today?'

She looked at him and smiled.

'How are *you* Tom,' she asked caringly.

He smiled.

'I'm good.'

She leaned over and gave him a hug almost capsizing Butterfly in the process. He laughed.

'*Oops!* I'd sit down if I were you,' he said with a warm smile. She sat down and looked up to the safety rail at the top of the embankment wall. A couple of tourists seeing that Lottie had almost capsized the boat, had clearly thought it amusing.

'Idiot,' she mumbled to herself.

'Oh I've been called worse,' said Tom with a grin.

'No no, not you To...' he interjected, 'I know Lottie. Let's push off.'

They set sail for Mill Pool.

They spoke very little during the sail. Lottie felt that Tom needed the quietude for reflection and memories of Grace and Tom's life together. There was just enough breeze to catch the sail. She had mentioned it before, but

Lottie told Tom again just how beautiful Butterfly looked in full sail, he knew of course, but appreciated the sentiment all the same. Even though she was quiet throughout, Tom was pleased that she had agreed to accompany him on such a poignant day.

At Mill Pool, whilst holding the cremation urn encasing Grace's ashes, Tom said a few emotive words, he then looked at Lottie and smiled kindly at her. She in turn passed him a considered and compassionate smile. He said his final goodbye to his sister and with loving care he slowly began to release the ashes into the river. They sat in silence together for a few minutes rocking to-and-fro in the gentle undulating swell of the current, before Tom spoke.

'Let's have that drink we promised each other the last time we were here.' He pointed to the Ferry Boat Inn.

She smiled tenderly and nodded her head.

'Yes. Let's. An orange juice for me please Tom.'

Lottie was sat on the quayside wall thinking about what she was going to say to Tom about the information she may have discovered, when Tom appeared carrying the drinks.

'Are you sure you didn't want a pint? It's a nice ale.'

She placed her hands on her hips.

'I hope you're not being sexist!'

His eyes widened as he placed the glasses down carefully on a flat stone on the edge of the wall; the only part of the path that isn't cobbled.

'I'm an emaciated woman I'll have you know.'

Tom narrowed his eyes questioningly. He wasn't sure whether she knew what she'd said or…she continued, 'and that should have been emancipated, before you make a glib comment.'

'I hadn't noticed.'

'Which means that you generally don't listen to me, or just now…here, today, as a one off?' She said with a purposeful and searching look. Which immediately gave way to an elfish grin.

Tom sat down next to her on the quayside wall.

'I'm so glad you came today Lottie. I think without you being here, it would have been quite difficult for me, and I think I would have been rather miserable.'

'What you have been through Tom, I think you are allowed to indulge in a little self-pity.'

'Well, I don't know about that Lottie. I've never been one for self-indulgence. Although, as I say, I would have felt more the sadder had you not have been here today to discuss the rather sensitive topic of emaciation.'

She laughed. He raised his glass in the direction of Mill Pool which is easily visible from where they were sat.

'To you Grace.'

Lottie raised her glass also.

'Grace.'

A short time passed and the handful of tourists that had been sat near them on the wall, had left. They were left on their own, which in itself was an infrequent occurrence as it is a very popular place for tourists and locals.

'I really enjoyed that orange juice,' said Lottie licking her lips.

'I noticed how quickly it went down. It hardly touched the sides,' said Tom with a hint of sarcasm.

'When I find something I like, there's no holding back.'

'Like Bakewell Tart.'

'Exactamundo!'

He laughed.

Just then a car towing a small boat, was being driven very cautiously down the slope and onto the small beach area in front of them, came to a halt. A young couple got out, walked round to the tow bar and uncoupled the boat. The man then got back in the car, turned it around and drove up the slope around the corner of the Ferry Boat Inn and disappeared. The young woman waited patiently for his return.

'On one occasion, I came here, 'said Tom, 'it was quite a high spring tide. When I approached the pontoon in Butterfly, I saw a car completely submerged under water,' he pointed to where the car had just left, 'virtually where that woman is standing now.'

'*No,*' she said with a slight scepticism.

'There is a sign,' he pointed to it, 'to be aware of the tides if parking on the beach here. But unfortunately there have been a few people who have sailed back here after a very pleasant day's sailing, only to find their car underwater.'

She laughed.

'Sorry Tom, I shouldn't laugh, but…you know. What a thing. It could really paint your rainbow grey.'

He smiled and nodded.

'Yes. And some. So, how's the commission coming along?'

She smiled broadly.

'Unusually good.'

'Do you normally struggle with your artwork?'

'I guess it's a bit like writing. You sometimes hit a wall or self-doubt creeps in.'

He paused briefly and looked earnestly at her.

'So then. What have you found Lottie?'

She looked at him with a slight hesitancy.

She let out a sigh.

'OK. I know that you went to Greece and France in search of Hellene, and that you had exhausted every avenue and it had come to nothing.'

He nodded his head.

'It was hopeless. I spoke to the few friends that I knew she had in London. I then went to Greece. I tried her Mother, father and her Greek friends and relatives. And then I went to look for her in Paris. I spoke to her relatives there and with everyone that I could find that knew her. Nobody had heard from her…it was as if she had disappeared. If it hadn't been for the letter, that's exactly the conclusion I would have come to, either that, or she was dead, which I didn't want to contemplate for Daisy's sake. In the end, I had to give it up Lottie. It was all consuming and beginning to affect Daisy. I was neglecting her and I couldn't allow that to happen, so I just stopped looking. But in my heart and mind…' he paused and looked at Lottie and then continued, 'well, you know the dust, it still floats all around me.'

Lottie sat and looked at him thoughtfully before continuing, 'it was something you said to me that was in the letter. Something that I think you had missed. I think that you were too close to it to see. I heard it from you and now have read it in the letter. I think she left you a clue Tom.'

'A clue? No Lottie. I have read the print off that letter. There is nothing in it, other than why she left me.'

'I think there is Tom.'

'What is it you think you've found?'

'It was the last line. The intonation of it just didn't sit right.'

'Intonation?'

'Yes. The tone or accent if you like didn't fit in with the rest of the letter.'

He sat deep in thought clearly going over the last line of the letter. Lottie removed the copy of the letter from her bag. She passed it to him. He scrutinised it, then let out a sigh.

'I don't see anything there Lottie.'

'You went to Paris in search of her. It was a reasonable assumption as that's where her father, most of his family and therefore, Hellene's relatives and friends were from.'

'Yes. That's correct. As far as I knew and from what they told me in Paris, they were all she knew. I believed them. I believed that they had not seen her or had any idea where she was. And the same can be said for the Greek side of her family. I believed them all to be genuine.'

'I think you're right. They didn't know where she was. Whatever her reason, or reasons, she wanted to start a new life without any ties to her past. She wanted to cut free from everything. In the letter, she said that she had fallen out of love; not that she wanted a whole new identity. But that's exactly what she did.'

'How do you know that Lottie. With all respect, and I know you are just trying to help me, but how can you come to that conclusion?'

'I don't think it was because she had stopped loving you Tom, I really don't. I think there was another reason. That's why she couldn't quite let go, and left a clue.'

He sighed again and shook his head.

'She didn't leave *anything* other than her daughter and me Lottie.'

She lifted up the letter and read out the last line,

'"Where I now choose to live out the rest of my life, will be my lot.",' she looked at him hoping that he would finally see what she had seen. She continued, 'she didn't go to Greece or Paris she went to a place where she had been ill as a child and had been cared for by a friend of her father's. A place where she had found peace and comfort.'

He looked totally perplexed.

'How do you know all this Lottie. Where did you get that information from?'

She looked at him and continued, 'when she wrote the words, "my lot", it wasn't my lot, as in my *lot* in life; she meant it was the *place* where she would live out the rest of her life...*Lot*, as in Lot-et-Garonne in France.'

'*What?*' he said in total bewilderment.

'Lot-et-Garonne.'

'What are you *saying* Lottie. That she walked away from everyone and everything that her life had ever been associated with? No. I appreciate what you're doing; but your wrong.'

'Whatever her reason for leaving you and Daisy, a part of her couldn't let go. Deep in her heart, she *wanted* you to find her, but her clue was *too* cryptic and you were too emotionally drained too unravel the sign. I'm so sorry Tom, but I'm certain that's where she went.'

Tom sat quietly, the silence only punctuated by the shouts of joy of two children on the pontoon as the huge crab they had hauled out, fell from the piece of bacon it had been gripping with its claw. It fell on the decking and they squealed and watched as it scrambled quickly sideways then with a "plop" back into the water.

'If what you say is correct. When I'd asked her father for the names of friends and relatives in France, he didn't mention this family friend in Lot-et-Garonne. Why would he leave that out?'

Lottie shook her head.

'I don't know Tom. Maybe it had been so long ago, that he'd simply forgotten; or the friend could have passed away. I don't know.'

'If she didn't leave us because she had fallen out of love with me, what would have driven her to do what she did? I'm more confused now Lottie than ever before.'

She stroked his arm tenderly.

'I'm so sorry Tom. I didn't do this to cause you more pain and confusion.'

He turned and looked kindly at her.

'I know Lottie...I know. I asked you to do this. So, please don't blame yourself. I'm now beginning to think that she might have had a breakdown of some kind,' he paused momentarily, 'I can't recall seeing any signs or symptoms of a psychological breakdown, I'm no psychiatrist of course, but I think there would have been something different in her emotions or behaviour. I would have known. I'm sure of that.'

Lottie remained silent and gave Tom a little space to go over and work through what he had just been told. A few minutes passed by wordlessly...

'Do you have an address in Lot-et-Garonne?'

She nodded her head slowly and thoughtfully.

'Yes. It's in a small village not far from Villeneuve-sur-Lot.'

He looked at her searchingly.

'How *ever* did you find this information in so much detail?'

'The internet: and a few other sources.'

'All this…on the internet.'

'Yes. More or less. Once I had figured out what she had meant by "lot" or Lot, I began a more detailed search. There are all kinds of records available on the internet; you would be shocked at the ease you can get very private and personal information and knowledge about people. We're really not safe you know.'

'Safe?'

'Everything about us is out there. Anyone who has the skill, can find out *anything* about *anyone*. If I can use it to find this information about Hellene without too much trouble; then god help us all in the future.'

'That's a bleak picture you're painting Lottie.'

'Yes it is Tom. That's exactly what it is.'

He let out a sigh. Lottie continued, 'you had given me her family name and I accessed the equivalent of our Census records. Not unlike the Germans, the French are meticulous record keepers. I was incredibly lucky. There she was, Hellene Dubois aged nine in Lot-et-Garonne or more precisely, the village of Nérac. You had told me that they were from Paris, so my first presumption was that they were on holiday, which they might well have been. But she fell ill.'

'How do you know she was ill and not just on holiday?'

'It was a leap of faith. I have to say.'

'A leap of faith? You are basing what you've told me, on a leap of faith? You don't have any real evidence to prove it?'

'No. Well, not exactly. However, Hellene was on the Census record on that night of the enumeration. Do you know what I mean by that?'

'Yes. I think so. If it follows the way our Census used to be taken, the register was taken at the same time, same day, right across the country and wherever you were, that's where you were recorded to be, not where you actually lived.'

'Yes, that's right. Only a Madame Alice Moreau aged fifty-eight, and one other was at that address that night.'

'Hellene.'

'Yes. Hellene Dubois.'

'It doesn't mean she was ill?'

'Then where were her parents?'

He scratched his head.

'I don't know Lottie.'

'So, with that leap of faith in mind, I set about finding the number of the local Doctor's surgery in the village, in the hope that what I was thinking, was on the right track.'

'Patient confidentiality. They wouldn't be allowed to give out any information.'

'Yes you're absolutely right. That's exactly what the receptionist said. I explained the reason for my request and gave her my number on the off chance that having heard the story, she might have a change of heart. It was a long shot; I have to say.'

Tom shook his head.

'No. They wouldn't do that. They wouldn't give out that kind of sensitive information.'

'And that's exactly what I thought. At that point, I'd hit a wall. There was nowhere else for me to go.'

'That point?'

'Yes. That point.'

'What happened?'

'A few days later, I received a call; the number wasn't recognised. I didn't answer. A few moments later I got a message notification. It was a Madame Bernard. She told me that her friend, the Doctor's receptionist, had been talking with her. She shouldn't have, but she mentioned the story to her. Madame Bernard remembered Madame Moreau who had passed away many years ago. She also remembered her taking in a little girl who had fallen ill with Chicken Pox. As Neither of the girl's parents had previously had Chicken Pox, there was a risk they could contract it and end up with Shingles. They found accommodation at a local B&B whilst the little girl fought the illness.'

'That little girl, was Hellene?'

'Yes it was Tom. Her parents hadn't left her at all. I just hadn't picked them up on the Census. I was too focussed on finding Hellene, that I didn't see them on the register. I simply missed them.'

'As you said, that's still a *huge* leap of faith, with the premise that that's where Hellene went when she walked away from us and left our lives that day.'

'Yes Tom. It is exactly that. But my feeling is that, that's where she went. She went back to a place of her childhood. A place where, although she was ill, she remembers that time as a healing; a place of comfort. I think it is a strong possibility.'

He sat deep in thought for a few moments before continuing, 'I want to go there; to Lot-et-Garonne. I think I have to Lottie.'
She nodded her head in agreement.
'I think you should.'
He smiled at her.
'You have done *amazingly* well to sift through all that information. Even if it doesn't lead to anything; thank you so much. I *really* do appreciate your help.'
She smiled affectionately.
'It's my pleasure Tom. After you had told me your story in Waterhead Creek, and I saw how you felt that day; how it has resonated through the years, and how it is still as raw now as it was then; the dust, the jigsaw puzzle...I wanted to do something; if I could.'
He returned a warm smile and sat quietly and reflectively for a few moments...

'Well, this Care in the Community thing, does it extend, if you have the time of course, to accompanying me on a visit to a lovely part of France?'
'When you sell it to me like that, how could I possibly refuse.'
He held out his arms to offer her a hug, which she accepted unconditionally. They released each other and

smiled amiably. Tom looked across to Mill Pool and sighed.

'Hell of a day, hey Lottie.'

'Not one you deserve Tom.'

'Life.'

'Life indeed.'

Once again he looked to where Grace's ashes had been scattered just a short time earlier.

'Today I've said farewell to Grace; but in some small way, Hellene may have been returned to me.'

'I do hope so Tom.'

'At the funeral, Grace in her will, had asked that I read a poem out for her. When I first read her request I was a bit taken-a-back to be honest. I didn't think that she took to poetry. But it is a lovely poem, and sitting here in this place, looking out to where she rests, the news of Hellene and the tranquillity of the river,' he paused smiled tenderly, nodded his head slowly up and down then continued, 'yeah. I see it now. I understand the meaning and significance of the words.'

'Who is it by?'

'Erm…Theodore Stephanides.'

'Do you remember the lines?'

'Yes. For an old wrinkly, I still have a good memory.' She laughed.

'You're not wrinkly. And you're *certainly* not old.' He laughed.

'I've more wrinkles than a walnut.'

'Don't talk like that Tom. It isn't true.'

'Anyway, I read and re-read the poem so that I wouldn't have to look at a sheet of paper at the funeral service. I think that always looks a little contrived and doesn't really appear that you've taken any time over it. I wanted to direct the words to the friends that had come to say their goodbye's to Grace. You can't really do that when you keep having to look down at a scrap of paper.'

'What's the poem called?'

'Departure.'

'Recite it Tom.'

'What?'

She smiled.

'Go on. Please.'

He owed her so much, how could he refuse her this small thing.

He looked around and about him, the nearest people were sat at a table near the ferry bell. He sat thoughtfully, gathering the words into the correct order...

'A part of us still lingers when we leave
A place that we have loved for many years,
In all its shapes of home and path and field,
Of wood and dell, of scent that follows rain,
Of everything down to the tiniest flower.

A part of us remains, and that half-self
Still wanders through those well-remembered ways;
Until sometimes we feel as if we were
A shade that alternates between two lives,
A ghost inhabiting two worlds, and yet
Not fully fleshed in either…'

He looked at Lottie. Tears were forming.
He smiled.
'Beautiful isn't it.'
She smiled and nodded.
'Yes Tom; it is,' she said in a hushed voice, 'I wish I'd met her.'
He smiled then let out a small laugh.
'Well she sure wanted to meet you.'
Lottie smiled companionably and linked him by the arm. They sat in silence looking out across the restful and peaceful river.

Tom was about to embark on a journey which would ultimately and finally lead to an explanation and give reason as to why a perfectly good and loving marriage and motherhood, would so dramatically come crashing down on that fateful day, in his, and Daisy's life. The answers to which, might possibly cause yet more sorrow and blameless, but unavoidable regret...

Chapter Sixteen

Bristol airport, 2 weeks later…

Tom pointed to the departures board.
'Bergerac. Right Lottie that's us then.'
They picked up their cabin bags and headed off down the terminal corridor to the departure gate. Within twenty minutes, they had boarded and the plane was on its way.

In just a little over two hours they landed at Bergerac airport.

They took a taxi for the small commune of Nérac in the Lot-et-Garonne and an hour and thirty-five minutes later they arrived at their hotel. It was late afternoon…

A knock came to Tom's door.

'Come in.'

It was Lottie.

'Nice rooms Tom. Good choice.'

'Indeed.'

'What do you fancy doing for the rest of the day?'

'I think we should get something to eat and then have a look around. It looks very pretty. A little adventuring, and begin the search tomorrow. What do you think?'

'Cool. Exactly what I had in mind.'

'How's your French?'

She gave a thoughtful frown.

'Not great. School girl French. I can get by though as long as they don't speak to quickly and run away with themselves. How about you?'

'I'm not too bad actually.'

'Oooo. Get you.'

'I had a little bit of the language under my belt as I had to come to France on and off on business. But when I married Hellene, and with her father being French, I made a big effort to impress him. I did a couple of short courses; holiday French you might call it, but I took to it really quickly. I found it quite easy to pick up.'

'You can order the food then.'

He laughed.

'It may well end up with us having to eat something that we didn't want, but asked for.'

'I kind of like that idea.'

'You're just odd.'

'I think that's the nicest thing you have ever said about me Tom.'

'It's a skill. I have a way with words.'

'I'll go and pull my Dock Martins on and I'll see you in about, say, twenty-minutes?'

'Yes. That'll give me time to slip into a nice evening dress.'

'I'm not sure why that excites me.'

'Bye Lottie,' he said in a rather camp manner.

She smiled broadly, and then laughed.

'See you later Tom.'

Thirty minutes later found them walking up Rue Séderie in the old town area where they found a nicely located restaurant by the Baïse River. Inside, they were directed to a table for two by a window with a river view.

'I do like rivers.'

She smiled.

'I know Tom.'

'I think I prefer rivers to the sea. The sea is nice enough but to me at least, rivers are more dynamic and ever changing. The current as it ebbs and flows, the way it changes the whole scene exposing mudflats and sandbanks and because they are restricted somewhat by their banks, the little boats that sail up and down them are easily seen and are so diverse. At sea it's such a vast space that you don't have that same closeness. Yes, the waves change form and shape, but…well, it's not the same.' He looked at her and smiled, 'just my opinion of course.'

'I can see what you're saying. I've never really compared them like that to be honest. But I agree with you about rivers. Where I used to live, a river ran through it. The Great Ouse.'

'Do you mean great as fabulous?'

She laughed.

'No. It's the River Great Ouse. Although, *yeah*, it *is* great

'I know Lottie. Just kidding.'

She sat back in her chair and narrowed her eyes.

'Hum. I think I remember a conversation about your knowledge of exactly which St Ives I lived in.'

His eyes widened.

'Errrm.'

The conversation was headed off by the waiter arriving at the table to take their order.

With the meal ordered and duly eaten, they took a walk along the riverbank where they came to a small café.

They sat at a table alfresco. Almost immediately a young woman appeared.

'Bonjour.'

'Bonjour,' they repeated in unison.

'Lottie?'

'Oh, I'd like a fresh orange juice please.'

Tom turned to the young woman, 'and could you choose a good local red wine for me?'

The waitress smiled.

'Of course. A small or large glass?'

'A large glass please.'

She smiled, turned and walked inside the café.

'Seems pleasant,' said Tom.

'Yes. Everyone we've met here seems friendly.'

'I do think the Brits have the wrong impression of the French.'

Lottie gave Tom an uncertain smile.

'Hmm, maybe sometimes yes.'

'What a lovely view.'

'Can't disagree with that.'

Tom looked at her. She was dressed in a way which was every inch the artist. Quirky yet understated. He really liked Lottie; her outlook on life, her dress sense, her sensitivities and her compassion. She did remind him very much of Daisy at times.

She smiled at him as he observed her.

'Are you OK Tom?'

'You remind me of Daisy…sometimes.'

Tom had not really talked about Daisy, and Lottie hadn't pursued it.

'Do I really Tom.'

'Yes you do.'

She gave him an affectionate smile.

'In what way?'

He took in a deep breath and exhaled slowly.

'Your bohemian way of looking at life.'

'Bohemian. *Oooo,* that's nice, I like the idea of that.'

'Daisy was similar in that way. Conformity didn't really sit well with her, and she didn't believe everything she heard. I don't mean she subscribed to conspiracy theories; but she questioned things.' He paused thoughtfully, 'I do miss those conversations and discussions. She could hold her own. I don't mean in an arrogant superior way; but intelligently informed decisions. She could always argue, well not argue exactly, but she could get her point across. She had a good soul and a big heart. I've said it before, but you would have been good friends I think.'

Lottie smiled but didn't reply, she left Tom to sit and reflect momentarily.

From behind them, the waitress appeared and placed the drinks on the table in front of them; she smiled and said, 'à votre santé.'

'Merci beaucoup,' replied Tom.

He raised his glass.

'Cheers Lottie.'

'To Daisy Tom.'

He smiled kindly.

'To Daisy...and the Avant-guard.'

She laughed.

'Yeah. To non-conformity.'

Tom replaced his glass and asked Lottie, 'if you don't mind me asking Lottie, did something happen in St Ives?'

She seemed a little surprised and expressed a slight hesitant caution.

'Happen? What do you mean?'

'Well it was just something you said a while ago that there was nothing there for you anymore.'

'Did I?'

'Yes. I think you said, "nothing to tie me there anymore and stress free" or something like that. It just came across as though,' he paused, 'oh never mind. I shouldn't be asking you, its none of my business Lottie.'

She looked at him again a little guardedly.

'You're right Tom something did happen in St Ives. I am not offended that you asked me, in any way whatsoever. I will explain it to you, but not yet Tom, if that's OK. The time here is about helping you to, as you said, acquire the right picture and finally, hopefully, place the pieces together.'

'Of course it's Ok Lottie. I shouldn't have asked you.'

He smiled affectionately.

'Thank you Tom. I really don't mind you asking me anything. You're are a good man Tom.'

He laughed.

'Whoa steady there.'

She smiled and nodded her head slowly and perceptively.

'You are.'

A little time passed by before the conversation took a turn towards the reason for the trip to France...

'One thing I don't understand Lottie.'

'*One*? I don't understand *most* things.'

He laughed. She continued, 'what is it you don't understand?'

'Why Hellene completely cut herself away from Daisy. That has always been painful for me to live alongside. How could a mother do that? I don't mean I'm bitter about it, but that part of it all, has been...well, you know.'

'Sometimes in life there seems to be no explainable reason for the decisions that people make. On the face of it, it doesn't make sense to anyone who is close to them. It's difficult to say when or why a perfectly ordinary mind of a seemingly perfectly ordinary person becomes so clouded, that reality and illusion, truth and falsehood become so indistinguishable that thought and reason becomes an empty stare.' Tom listened attentively in silence as she continued, 'quite possibly the person has had a mental breakdown or maybe, there is a reason that goes beyond explanation.'

'Beyond explanation?'

'Yes. That it is so life-changing to that person, that if it were disclosed, it would greatly affect others, and so, the answer at that crucial moment in their life, is that they just disappear.'

Tom's brow furrowed questioningly.

'You think that something dire could have happened to Hellene, something so dreadful that she couldn't tell me? So she took it with her. I mean what could that possibly be?'

She smiled affectionately, and looked kind-heartedly at Tom.

'Hopefully we will get some kind of answer tomorrow.'

The die was cast, and as Tom had hoped, the following day he was to find answers that would bring about a conclusion, that for too long, has been such a hurting perplexity for him.

Chapter Seventeen

Having breakfasted at the hotel, the woman at the reception desk had ordered them a taxi to take them to the address Lottie had been given by Madame Bernard; the address of the late Madame Moreau. The hope was that whoever was living there now, might have some knowledge or clue to the whereabouts of Hellene.

The taxi took 20 minutes to reach the address. It was a pretty village with typical part timber framed, cruck houses of the Nouvelle-Aquitaine region. They paid the taxi driver, walked across the small road and approached the front door. Tom knocked on the door. The house frontage was cloaked in wisteria which had been carefully trained to follow the shape of the windows, framing them in a kind of floral portrait.
The door opened and a middle-age woman appeared. She gave them both an easy smile.
'Bonjour.'

Tom replied.

'Bonjour. Parlez vous anglais?'

She looked a little muddled.

'Er non.'

He was just about to test out his holiday French on her when the woman held up her finger and smiled, she turned, called out, '*Sophie.*' Within a few moments a young teenage girl appeared. She smiled at Tom and Lottie and then looked at her mother. Her mother asked Sophie to translate.

'Can I help you?'

Tom gave her a slightly ambiguous smile.

'We are trying to locate a young girl who lived here many years ago with a Madame Moreau.'

She turned to her mother and translated. The mother shrugged her shoulders and spoke to Sophie.

'My mother doesn't remember a Madame Moreau. How long ago was it that she lived here?'

'It was nineteen-sixty. She was Ten years old.'

The girl translated. This time the woman raised her hands and gave a more animated but apologetic shrug of her shoulders. She spoke to the girl.

'My mother said that there has been another family here at this house before we came. She...' her mother interrupted, and pointed to an old farm house. The young girl continued, 'Madame Caron who lives there may remember Madame Moreau. Her family own the farm over there,' she pointed to some fields that lay behind the house. 'they have lived and farmed there for many generations. She might remember something.'

Tom smiled at the woman.

'Merci beaucoup Madame.'

The woman smiled benevolently and nodded her head. Tom continued, 'thank you so much.'

'I should come with you. Madame Caron speaks very little English,' she gave an impish grin and continued, 'she can...but she won't.'

Lottie laughed. Sophie's mother asked her what Lottie had laughed about; Sophie just shook her head and said it was nothing. She told her mother that she was going with Lottie and Tom to Madame Caron's. Her mother nodded her head and smiled.

'Au revoir et bonne chance.'

Lottie smiled.

'Merci beaucoup Madame. Au revoir.'

The girl led Tom and Lottie across to Madame Caron's house. She took them around the back to a cobbled courtyard.

'*Madame Caron.*'

'*Oui.*' A woman appeared.

Madame Caron is a squat older lady with a low centre of gravity, she has sharp, clear and almost piercing blue eyes, which swam with knowledge. Sophie explained why Tom and Lottie were there. Madame Caron thought carefully for a short time, then a perceptible recollection. She spoke with Sophie once again. The conversation and animated gesturing between them both, seemed to Lottie and Tom to be endless. Eventually Sophie spoke to them.

'OK. So, she does remember Madame Moreau and the little girl. She was ill and Madame Moreau had looked after her. She can't remember her exactly though; it was so long ago. She does recall her being a very pleasant girl.'

'Hellene,' said Tom nodding his head in acceptance.

Unexpectedly, the woman smiled and clapped her hands, '*Oui oui*. Hellene. Hellene Dubois.'

Tom looked at Lottie, 'Dubois was Hellene's maiden name.'

'I know Tom. You told me, remember.'

He gave her a deeply meaningful, congratulatory smile. 'Well done you.'

Lottie returned a contented, yet slightly curious and cautious smile.

Madame Caron then continued speaking rather excitedly to Sophie. Once again the conversation seemed limitless.

'OK. So, as soon as you said the name Hellene, she remembered a conversation she'd had with a friend a few years ago at the local market about Hellene and Madame Moreau. The friend had known Madame Moreau and had met the girl. She had told Madame Caron that about forty-eight years ago,' she paused to confirm the number of years with Madame Caron, she nodded her head, and said a few words to Sophie, then Sophie continued, 'yes she confirms it was about that, she had seen Hellene, who was now of course a woman. She recognised her by a petite, but recognisable birthmark under the right hand side of her chin.'

Tom let out a sigh, looked directly at Lottie and nodded his head slowly in the conclusion that it must have been Hellene. Sophie continued, 'she later discovered that erm,' she paused and looked at Tom questioningly, 'Hellene?' He nodded his head and she continued, 'that Hellene was living in the next village to here. To this village.'

Tom's eyes widened.

'Is Madame Caron's friend still alive?'

Sophie turned and spoke with Madame Caron. Madame Caron answered and then laughed out loud.

Sophie could see that Tom's situation seemed to be a rather desperate one and not really the right moment for humour. Sophie gave Madame Caron a pacifying look.

'I'm sorry that the Madame laughed, she said yes she is still alive and so is she, and she intends to out live her friend.'

Tom smiled kindly at Madame Caron.

'Do you have an address of Madame Caron's friend,' asked Lottie with an oddly fixed, unemotional stare which Tom picked up on. Sophie turned, and spoke once more to Madame Caron.

'Yes. But she said that it might be better if she phoned her first.'

Tom and Lottie nodded in agreement. Madame Caron spoke to Sophie, Sophie smiled and pointed to a table and chairs, 'she said we can sit here whilst she speaks with her friend.'

A little time passed before Madame Caron came back to the courtyard. Although Tom and Lottie could speak a little French, neither of them could quite get a handle on the dialect. She spoke to Sophie. Sophie's demeanour changed to one that showed a little perplexity. She seemed to be questioning something that Madame Caron had said. When it had been confirmed, she continued, 'Madame Caron's friend lives about fifteen minutes walk from here. I could come with you, show you where it is, and translate if you need me to?'

Tom and Lottie agreed without question.

'That would be very kind of you, if you're sure you don't mind?'

Sophie smiled.

'I don't mind at all. I think I should go with you,' she said a little cryptically.

After fifteen minutes they arrived at the house. The door opened...she was expecting them. The lady said hello to Tom, Lottie and Sophie, she then spoke to Sophie at length. During the conversation Sophie kept glancing furtively at Tom and Lottie.

'OK. She does confirm that it was Hellene,' she gave a thoughtful pause. 'however, she doesn't live here anymore.'

Tom looked down in a slight despondency. He looked up and asked Sophie, 'does she have any idea where she is now Sophie?'

'She went back to England.'

'Back to *England?*' he repeated in a disorientation. 'When?'

'She recalls that it was nineteen-ninety-two.'

'That's very precise Sophie. How can she be so sure?'

Sophie looked at Tom apologetically.

'She left after her daughter had died.'

Tom's face drained of blood. He went so pale that Lottie felt he would feint. He was totally and utterly confused with what Sophie had just said.

'That can't possibly be Sophie,' he said in a whispered voice, 'Hellene's daughter was my daughter and she lived with me in England. She died *in* England. The Madame must be confused.'

Sophie spoke once again with the woman. Both Tom and Lottie could see that the woman showed absolutely no doubt that it was Hellene and Hellene's daughter. Sophie looked once more apologetically at them both. The woman spoke again and pointed beyond the village.

'She said that the girl was about eighteen when she died and she is buried in a cemetery that is not too far away from here. It is about ten minutes by car. The woman spoke again.

'She said if you would like to go to the cemetery her grandson, who is here in the house, could take you?'

Tom and Lottie both agreed. Tom looked at Lottie she looked solemnly sad. He held her arm.

'It's OK Lottie whatever we find there...it's alright, honestly. Please don't get too disheartened for me. I'm getting close now Lottie. I feel that.'

She smiled affectionately.

They thanked and said goodbye to Sophie and the Madame and within ten minutes they were at the cemetery gates.

'Would you like me to wait for you?' asked the young man.

'No thank you so much for bringing us here. That's very thoughtful of you. Do you perhaps have the telephone number of a taxi, so that we can get back to our hotel?'

'Yes of course.' He scrolled through his contacts and read out a number. Lottie stored it in her phone. They said goodbye, and walked through the cemetery gates. There wasn't a soul about and there seemed to be no one in or around the caretaker's lodge.

They walked slowly and respectfully around and in amongst the grave stones.

After just over half-an hour of searching they found the grave. The inscription was a simple one:

CATHERINE DUBOIS
(1974-1992)
TAKEN TOO SOON.
MAY YOU REST IN PEACE.

Tom couldn't take in what he was seeing.

'She had a child? She had another daughter Lottie. Why didn't she tell me? Whatever it was, I would have understood. Why Lottie?' He turned and looked at Lottie. Stood quietly and motionless, she had tears streaming down her face.

'What is it Lottie?'

'I have waited so long for this moment Tom. For so long I have tried desperately to find her.'

Tom was bewildered.

'I don't understand what you're saying Lottie?'

She drew in a deep breath.

'My name,' she looked at Tom dolefully, 'my name is Lottie Dubois. Catherine (Kitty) Dubois was my mother.' She reached out and touched the headstone lovingly, and still gently weeping, she went down on to her knees.

Tom was utterly and completely bewildered. He couldn't comprehend what had just unfurled, and although his thoughts were in freefall, he did however, have the presence of mind to kneel down beside her and put his arm around her shoulder to comfort her: on doing so, she began to sob uncontrollably.

After a few moments she fought back the tears and became a little calmer which enabled her to speak to Tom, 'I never knew where she was Tom. I had no idea. Like you with Hellene; the not knowing is the cruellest and painful of all emotions. You can come to terms with

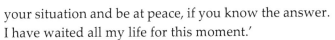

your situation and be at peace, if you know the answer. I have waited all my life for this moment.'

He helped her to her feet and then walked her over to a bench. They sat in silence together: Tom trying to work out exactly what this disclosure meant, and Lottie, after so long, finally coming to terms with the loss of her mother, Kitty. The more Tom analysed what had happened, the clearer it became.

'I know that this isn't the best time to ask you, but do you feel that you can tell me now Lottie? Is Hellene still alive?'

She looked at him and smiled affectionately, but apologetically.

'I hope that you will understand and find it in your heart to forgive me for what I'm about to say to you and reason why I haven't told you what little I already knew. And I *do* feel guilty for that Tom. More than I can say.'

'I am a little hurt Lottie I have to be honest with you, and I do feel a little betrayed at this moment in time; but I just want to know what happened Lottie...that's all I have ever wanted for Daisy and me. The truth.'

She held his hand.

'Hellene died on the eighteenth of March this year.'

'Oh sweet Jesus.' Tom lifted up his head and closed his eyes. 'My dear Hellene,' he repeated in a hushed voice. Once again the tears began to roll down Lottie's cheeks. She lowered her head and held it in her hands.

'I am so *sorry* Tom.'

He stroked the back of her head lovingly.

'It's alright Lottie.'

'It's not alright Tom. It is *not* alright. I didn't know what to do.'

Tom trying to hold back his tears continued, 'tell me Lottie. Tell me what happened.'

She composed herself and stared at her mother's grave. 'When I told you that my mother died when I was young; she died in childbirth. Her life was ended by giving life to me. That guilt stays with you. It haunts you. People tell you that it's not your fault; that there was nothing anyone could do, but you *do* blame yourself.' She looked affectionately at Tom and continued, 'I knew nothing about you, my mother, Daisy or even who my father was. As I told you, Hellene, my grandmother, would never discuss anything precisely to do with her past. In October last year, she found a small lump in her breast. It was diagnosed as an aggressive cancer and had already spread. It was terminal. She was hospitalised for a short time. Then she was allowed to come home for her final few days. She was cared for so beautifully by the Macmillan nurse. I really don't know how I could have coped without her support. I stayed by her bedside day and night, until the end. Although she was full of morphine and not suffering, because of the medication she did become incoherent and a little rambling. It was about 4am when she woke me by touching my arm. She made me jump. She looked at me and her eyes were as clear as a child's. She said sorry to me for all the mistakes she had made. She apologised for not talking to me about my mother, her family and her past. She told me that you were away on an engineering project when, and she didn't go into detail, when she had an "indiscretion". Something she regretted until the end. She fell pregnant with Kitty, my mother. She thought that it would be too painful for her husband, you Tom, to hear the truth, so she lied and gave up everything she loved, so as not to hurt you or stigmatise her daughter she'd had with you…Daisy. She wasn't thinking clearly and although she had hidden it very well from you, her mental state of mind wasn't good. In her disordered mind, and not being able to think straight, she thought that by saying in the letter, that she had left you because she had stopped loving you; that maybe you would get angry and the pain of that would pass more quickly than the truth and hurt of what had actually happened.' She looked at Tom; he sat quietly and did not interrupt her. She continued, 'I felt so so sorry for her Tom. She was just about to tell me about my mother when her body suffered a huge spasm. I could see she was wracked with pain as it tore through her.' Lottie's eyes began to fill once again with tears.

'Do you want to stop Lottie?'

'No Tom. There has been silence and secrets for too long. I reached for the morphine, she shook her head and said, "no. Not yet my darling." I remember that moment of brave selflessness so clearly. She knew that if she had taken more morphine, she would not be able to finish what she had to say; the words that should have been said all those years ago. She told me that my

221

mother was buried in France, but, as hard as she tried, she couldn't recall exactly where. I think because she was in so much agonising pain; her mind had clouded over. I wanted to push her and ask her directly where she was buried, I was so desperate at that moment. I knew that if she died then; I would *never* find my mother. She was my only hope, and she was slipping away. But I couldn't ask her; how could I do that. I let her rest for a few moments. Then, quite unexpectedly and with great clarity, she told me more about you. She said your name - Tom Derham, and that you lived in Dartmouth in Devon. She was so confused by now, and had forgotten what she had only just told me; so it was all a little jumbled up but she said that her daughter was called Daisy and that she loved you both more than words could ever say. She then went on to tell me again the reason why she had left you and Daisy. She was, by now, *so* confused. Her body started to shake with the pain and I had to give her the morphine. I *had* to do that Tom. I never did find out where my mother was buried. Hellene passed away peacefully at just passed six-o'clock that morning. She was such a brave soul Tom, a courageous woman who loved you both until she fell into a final peace.'

Once again Tom put his head back and this time, he cried. Lottie comforted him as best she could. She gave him some silent space...there were no more words. Sometimes, it's the space between words that has more meaning.

Several minutes passed by in quietude as they both absorbed what the truth had finally given up.

Lottie was first to speak.
'I didn't know what to do Tom. I found you in the Dartmouth directory. Then I remembered that an old university friend lived near Kingswear. I looked up the address and saw that it was located near to Dartmouth. I looked for her number, and I still had it. I gave her a call. I didn't lie when I told you that I was house sitting for her. It was incredibly good timing. They were looking for someone to housesit for them. After I'd moved in, I found out where you lived and passed your house several times in the hope that I could catch a glimpse of you, either leaving or arriving at your house. Then a couple of days later, purely by chance, I was walking up School steps when I saw you sat on your balcony. The day after that, I was making my way to Bayard's Cove, when I saw you waiting for the ferry. It was the morning that you went to see Daisy; the first time we met. I didn't know where you were going of course, but I wanted to learn more about you...as much as I could. I just made it onto the ferry. You didn't notice me as you were looking across to Kingswear. I followed at a distance as you walked along Brixham Road. Luckily for me you didn't turn around once. I then followed you into the cemetery. And, well, you know the rest. Although Hellene had told me that her daughter with you was called Daisy, she had no idea, and neither did *I* until I saw you at her graveside, that

Daisy had died. I'd like to think that it was a blessing for Hellene not knowing, but I think the pain for her knowing that she would never see her again, was just as cruel. That in a sense, Daisy was already lost to her. It was so hard that day when we first met for me to keep all my emotions at bay. I couldn't give any thing away. The slightest hint of knowledge through a reaction or response and, well, I couldn't let that happen. Before I phoned you to meet up for a coffee, I had to be absolutely clear about what I was to do next. I was still uncertain whether to tell you there and then what I already knew. Was it the right thing to do at that moment? I wasn't certain and it was all very unclear. For some reason, I hesitated. It was when we were sat in Warfleet Creek and you told me that you had been searching for Hellene and that *you* wanted to find the answers, that I knew what I should do next. I would *help* you, not *tell* you; it was for you to discover as much of the truth that you could, with my help. I knew about my grandmother, Hellene, but I still had no idea about my mother. It wasn't until you told me about the letter, that I knew that's where we should go. For you to discover what had happened to Hellene and for me to find where my mother's remains lay. By leaving that one clue, and I'm certain of this Tom, Hellene had more or less said that she wanted you to find her. But as I said to you…the clue was too well hidden. I tried every record I could in France to find where my mother was buried,' she paused and looked towards the grave, 'I could find *no* record. Of course, I was searching for

Kitty Dubois not Catherine. I just never thought. I don't know why it didn't occur to me that Kitty could be short for Catherine. Also, it may have been easier and narrowed the search down a little more, if we didn't have the ubiquitous French name of Dubois.'

Tom continued to sit in silence before speaking out,' I am *so* sorry that you have had to carry that by yourself Lottie. What a cross to bear. Never knowing anything about your mother, your family or who your father is. Living as I have done with the devastating loss of not having Hellene in my life and then the death of my daughter at such an early age; I do understand what it is to have the strength of character to carry on when some days, all you want it to do…is end. We are both the same you and I Lottie, in many respects.'

'I hope you don't hate me for not telling you straight away Tom when we first met. I hope you can find it in your heart to forgive me. I did what I thought would be the best for both of us.'

He smiled lovingly at her.

'You have made me walk taller Lottie. You have brought light into my life where shadows and silhouettes once fell. I could *never* hate you.'

'Do you forgive me? I needed you to be there with me when I discovered my mother's final resting place. You were the only family left to me. There was no one else, and I didn't want to be on my own. Was that selfish of me Tom?'

'No. It wasn't. And there is *nothing* to forgive. You did it, I believe, through love and compassion. I will never be able to thank you enough for what you have done for me. Where there was confusion and misunderstanding, you have brought clarity and peace into my life. I remember the first time I saw Hellene in the café bar on that Greek island. That very first moment when I looked at the side of her face. My thoughts and those words I told you, are unaltered by anything that happened or anything that has been said since. I feel the same way about her now, possibly *more* so, now that I have the truth, than I did that day on that island, so long ago.'

Once again they sat in a reflective stillness.

Then Tom stood and walked a few paces. He stooped and picked a wildflower. He continued to do the same, picking flowers from around the cemetery. He brought them back to Lottie, and handed them to her. She smiled tenderly. She stood and walked over to her mother's grave. As Tom had done at Daisy's grave the day Lottie and Tom first met, gently and lovingly, she laid them at the the base of her mother's headstone.

'I'll come back and visit you mum...I promise. You were once lost, and now you are found. I love you so very much. Be at peace now.

They spoke very little on the way back home. They parted with the most heartfelt, affectionate and meaningful embrace.

A few days later, they left together for St Ives; for Tom to lay some flowers on Hellene's grave and to say the words to her that he could never have said, if it hadn't been for Lottie. And for Lottie to lovingly touch her grandmother's headstone once again.

On their return home, they had agreed to give each other some space; a little time to reflect on what had happened; the past, the present and the future, with the promise to each other that they would meet up again, soon...

Chapter Eighteen

Two weeks had passed since their return from St Ives. Tom had finalised a few business interests which had in turn realised a substantial amount of capital. He had been out socialising with his friends and had knocked a few drinks back with his friend the skipper of the Carlina. He had also, taken out Butterfly for a few trips up and down river.

Lottie had been busy finishing off her commission, and taking the occasional walk down Greenway Road to where it terminates at the little café on the quayside. There she would sit for an hour or two sipping coffee and reflecting. For the first time in her life she was at ease with herself, and the World.

Tom had just got out of the shower and was in his bedroom, when his phone rang. He just got to it before it rang off…it was Lottie.

'Hello Lottie. Strange. I was just thinking about you.'

'Oh yes,' she said sassily, 'something weird and Avant-guard I hope.'

He laughed.

'It is so good to hear your voice.'

'And yours Tom.'

'How have you been?'

'OK. I've been fine. I've finished that commission I was working on, which is just as well as I have to clear off shortly. My friend Toni has decided to return home early from traveling.'

There was a perceptible disappointment in Tom's voice.

'Where will you go?'

'Well, if I can afford it, I'll stick around. Maybe not Dartmouth or Kingswear; couldn't afford those prices. But I'll find somewhere.'

'Well if I can help in *any* way.'

'Thanks Tom. I appreciate that.'

'It is strange though. I was thinking this morning.'

'Do you not normally think in the morning?' she replied with a quip.

'I've also missed that sense of humour of yours.'

You mean cultured and well-timed?'

'No. I don't.'

She laughed.

'How do you feel about a few days away?'

'With you you mean?'

'No with a complete stranger.'

'Hmm that might be interesting.'

'With me Lottie.'

She laughed.

'I know. I think that would be a lovely idea Tom. Where do you have in mind?'

'It's not too far away and doesn't involve a plane.'

'OK. I'll pack a small case. When?'

'How about next Monday?'

'Monday's good.'

'Monday to Wednesday.'

'Yep. Sounds good.'

'Could you come here to the house?'

'Oh *hello*. You're not inviting me to stop over at your place are you Tom? What *would* the neighbours say?'

'No.'

'Well that was rather blunt and to the point. So then. That implies that wherever you're taking me is on your side of the river.'

'Possibly. Possibly not.'

'You like being all vague and interesting don't you Tom.'

'If you're not living on the edge, you're taking up too much room.'

'Oooo, nice respond there. One of yours?'

'No.'

'Are we going across the Channel?'

'Lottie.'

'OK. I'll stop guessing.'

'Good.'

'I'll park up in the Marina and meet you at yours. What time?'

'Around three pm.'

'Cool. Beard?'

'Shut yer face,' he said jauntily.

She gave a hearty laugh, which was followed by a short pause…

'I've missed your company Tom. I mean that.'

'Yes. Same here Lottie. Things are very different now for both of us. The course of lives has been altered somewhat I guess.'

'Yes it has Tom.'

'Right then. See you Monday Lottie.'

'Yes. See you then Tom. Looking forward to it. Bye.'

'Me too. Bye Lottie.'

Chapter Nineteen

July

Tom's doorbell rang. It was Lottie.

'I'm so sorry Lottie.'

She looked puzzled.

'What do you mean? Has something happened?'

Now Tom looked puzzled.

'Happened?'

'Why are you apologising?'

Then the realisation of the misinterpretation of his apology.

'No no. I'm sorry that I didn't pick you up from the ferry.'

'Why would you do that?'

'Your case.'

'Oh…right! It's really light and look,' she pointed at the wheels, 'it's very modern; it has, *wheels*,' she said with a playful sarcasm.

'Right. OK.'

She leaned across and gave him a kiss on both cheeks. Realising that it wasn't really enough, she put out her arms to hug him. He reciprocated. As he looked over her shoulder, he noticed Claire at her bedroom window. He gave her a small wave. Lottie turned and saw Claire. She also waved. Claire gave them both a warm smile. Although Tom hadn't discussed with anyone what had happened or what the situation was with them both, Claire had taken to Lottie on their first meeting, and the smile was honest and genuine.

'Are you good to go now Lottie or would you like a coffee or use the loo or…'

'Use the loo?'

He shrugged his shoulders.

'Well…you know.'

'As yet, I don't have incontinence. How about you Tom.'

'Well my pipework isn't what it used to be.'

She raised her eyebrows

'I think we should go.'

'Yes. Maybe I should have said bathroom, not loo.'

She smiled and nodded her head slowly but meaningfully in a matronly manner.

'Right then,' he said sheepishly.

His case was in the small hallway. Everything was turned off and closed up. He picked up his case and closed the door behind him.

The further he drove the more certain she became about the destination, and why.

Tom parked the car; they unloaded their suitcases and walked the few steps to The Beachfront Apartments which had formally been, The Torcross Hotel.
Tom had chosen well. The apartment was light and spacious with a balcony, which has panoramic views across the full length of Slapton Sands and out into the bay.

They spent the rest of the afternoon eating and walking along the sands.

Later that evening found them sitting together on the balcony: Tom with a glass of wine and Lottie with a fresh orange juice.

'This is so lovely Tom; I can't tell you.'
'I think you just did.'
'It was a figure of speech, not literal.'
'Even so.'
'I think I prefer you when your giving a history lesson rather than English elucidation.'
'Oh. It's been a while since I've enjoyed a good elucidate.'

234

'Yeah I can believe that.'

They both laughed.

There was a little pause…

'I was thinking the other day Tom, and I hope you don't mind me talking about Hellene?' He smiled sincerely and nodded his approval. She continued, 'as I'm Hellene's granddaughter, does that kind of make me…'

Tom interjected, 'yes Lottie, I have been thinking the same. I am your grandfather, of sorts at least, through marriage.'

She beamed a smile.

'You have *no* idea how over the last few days I have struggled as to whether I should ask you that.'

'You don't mind the thought of that?'

'No,' she said with absolute clarity. 'That makes me so happy…to know that I have family again.'

'On the other hand, don't feel that you have to call me grandad,' he said rather modestly.

'No. You will always be Tom. It's just nice to know that…well, as I said, the feeling of belonging once again, is to me, *so* wonderful.'

'Family, *is* everything Lottie,' he paused momentarily, stood and walked inside the apartment. He returned carrying a small package. 'I was going to do this tomorrow. But now seems appropriate.' He opened it to reveal a small bundle of brown twigs all the same length and thickness. There was also a piece of green garden twine. The twigs were about six inches long and a quarter of an inch in diameter. He looked at her and smiled; she returned a puzzled wry grin.

'What's this about then?'

He picked up one of the twigs.

'If I have a single twig,' he held it in front of him and snapped it in two, 'I can break it easily.' He then took the twine and tied the rest of the twigs tightly together and continued, 'if I try to snap them now,' as hard as he tried he couldn't break them, 'they are impossible to break.' He looked at her affectionately and continued, 'that's family.'

She smiled tenderly.

'That's so beautiful Tom.'

'I can't remember where I first heard it...but I never forgot it.'

She smiled again and nodded her head slowly. Then her eyes widened and she raised her eyebrows.

'And I, have something for you.'

She stood, and went inside the apartment. After a few moments she returned to the balcony. In her hand was a scroll of paper about the size of an A4 sheet.

'For you Tom.'

'For me?'

Carefully he unrolled the scroll.

'Oh my word.' It was Lottie's portrait of Tom that she had promised to give him when finished.

'It's just right Lottie. Thank you so much.'

She gave him an impish grin.

'I should *think* so too.' Then her smile became a little more heartfelt, 'it's my pleasure Tom.'

She sat quietly for a few moments deep in thought; there was something else she had to tell him.

'I have some news Tom.'

He tipped his head slightly in a questioning manner.

'What is it Lottie?'

'I'm pregnant.'

Tom's eyes widened perceptibly and a wide smile broke across his face.

'That's *wonderful* Lottie. I'm *so* happy for you,' he paused momentarily, 'you haven't really mentioned that you have a partner.'

'That's because I don't.'

'Right.'

'I'm so happy to be having a child, but what I don't really want or need right now, is a man in my life.' She looked at him, and she knew what he was thinking.

'Yes Tom. Talk about history repeating itself,' she said with a wry smile. She was of course referring to her mother, Kitty.

'You can't go wrong with bit of history,' he said tongue-in-cheek. 'If you don't mind me asking, do you know if it's a boy or a girl; or is it too soon to tell?'

She beamed a gratified smile.

'A girl. And she'll be called,' she looked deep into Tom's eyes and smiled warmly, 'Catherine Derham-Dubois. Or alternatively, I'd be quite happy if you call her Kitty.'

A huge broad, contented smile, set across Tom's face. She leaned across and hugged him and then sat back into her chair.

Tom knew exactly what should be offered to Lottie and what he should say next.

'I don't know how you would feel about living with an old man. But I would be more than happy to share my, rather *large* home, with you and Catherine…Kitty. If you think that it might work for you? You don't have to give me an answer now. Have a think about it. Take as much time as you need.'

'Tom. I can't think of anything I would like better than that. I honestly can't. I would be so grateful.'

'That's done then. You can stay as long as you wish. Come and go as you please; have friends round and I will never interfere with, or cramp your style in any way.'

She smiled affectionately at Tom.

'You enrich my existence Tom; you could never reduce it.'

Tom breathed in and let out a sigh slowly.

'I am *so* happy that you entered my life Lottie. You have brought me clarity and serenity. I am content with my little existence. And now that you are a part of my life, it feels complete. You have given me the true picture to the jigsaw puzzle, which has finally allowed the dust to settle.'

She leaned across and hugged him again for a few moments then gently released him.

Tom and Lottie's searching was over. The years of uncertainty and vagueness; behind them now. This however, is not the end of their story; it is the beginning…

They sat in the quietude and stillness of the night, listening to the calming, gently lapping waves as they washed up on to the shoreline, and looking out across the moonlit bay, and as Lottie had wished for, a big sky, a sky, so full of stars...

In silence, as I sat and looked
at her across the café bar,
I wondered if the left-hand side of her face,
could possibly be any
more beautiful than her right.

The settling of the dust

In memory of Jason (Jay) Wickenden
(1974-2018)
Skipper of the Carlina, Dartmouth

Printed in Great Britain
by Amazon